BE MY V
VAMPIRE

**Roses are red, violets are blue…
this Valentine's Day let a vampire seduce you!**

BE MY VALENTINE,
VAMPIRE

by

Michele Hauf
Cynthia Cooke
Vivi Anna
Theresa Meyers
Lisa Childs

Mills & Boon, an imprint of Harlequin (UK) Limited,
Eton House, 18-24 Paradise Road, Richmond, Surrey TW9 1SR

BE MY VALENTINE, VAMPIRE © Harlequin Books S.A. 2012

The publisher acknowledges the copyright holders of the individual works as
follows:

Vampire's Tango © Michele Hauf 2010
A Night with a Vampire © Cynthia D. Cooke 2011
Her Dark Heart © Vivi Anna 2010
Salvation of the Damned © Theresa Meyers 2009
The Secret Vampire Society © Lisa Childs-Theeuwes 2009

ISBN: 978 0 263 89716 6

024-0212

Printed and bound by
CPI Group (UK) Ltd, Croydon, CR0 4YY

CONTENTS

VAMPIRE'S TANGO

Michele Hauf

CHAPTER ONE

HE CLASPED my hand and placed his other hand at my bare back. Commanding fingers pressed firmly against my spine and sought to direct my movement. My skin sizzled at the connection.

I ignored the illicit response and met his eyes.

Dark and serious, his irises drew me into a sultry realm of the unknown. Yet they didn't ask anything more than "Will you follow?"

The bandoneón, an Argentinean accordion, pressed out notes. The violin sang. The singer wearing a black fedora enticed us into the tango.

The milonga, a tango club in underground Paris, was dark and smoky, reeking of whiskey, perspiration and clove cigarettes. Dancers clung to one another in various stages of the dance, some close as lovers, others holding an open embrace and learning their partner's movements as they taught him or her their own.

I was thankful my new partner held me in an open embrace that didn't allow for direct chest contact as we stepped to the beat around the floor. I followed the subtle direction of his eyes, his fingers and his steps.

I had been following him for two weeks around the tight, twisting Parisian streets.

Tonight was the first time I'd allowed him awareness of my presence.

This tenuous first connection slowly gained confidence as he held my hand sure, but not too tightly. I answered by following dutifully. He was taller than me by a head but he bent slightly at the knee, which brought him to my level. His cinnamon scent was appealing. The presence of his muscled body, completely focused on the dance, was overwhelming.

Altogether, much more enticing than I had expected the man to be.

A showy couple mastered the middle of the floor. We moved counterclockwise around the dance floor, flowing with the other dancers who had no need for grandstanding.

I knew his name: Alexandre Renard.

He would never know mine if I danced this tango of two opposites correctly. I was nervous about this physical link tonight, but determined.

The beat paused and he drew me closer, moving his face aside my cheek, but he didn't press his skin against mine. As it was, the proximity of our mouths felt dangerous. His hot breath brushed my lips. His fingers at my spine bent, moving me closer until our chests touched. We stood in the close embrace similar to those I'd determined were lovers.

I couldn't let him smell my fear. I'd doused myself with my favorite vanilla cherry essential oil this evening. But I knew it wouldn't matter. Fear could be felt.

I was not afraid. Perhaps, secretly cocky. The mark stood in my arms. All six foot two of him, clad in a sleek black suit and red silk tie. Dark hair slicked back from his masculine bone structure emphasized his fierce demeanor.

I slid my hand up his arm and around behind his neck, silently reassuring him this close hold was all right by me.

He turned abruptly, and walked forward. I followed, noting the subtle rebuff and projecting the surprising anger I felt in the force of my steps. He clutched me close, his hand high across my back and gripping my side, just under my arm.

We stepped the *baldoso*, back, side, forward twice, aside and then back to the embrace. A slide of his foot between my legs, was answered by a *gancho* as I hooked my leg about his. After the fight, the making up.

But we didn't make up for long, and I preferred it that way.

Turning swiftly, we glided past the musicians. The brush of his pin-striped coat teased at me through the thin black chiffon dress I wore. Everything about him intruded upon my external defenses. My clothing, my skin—but he would not penetrate my determination.

Palm to palm, hip-to-hip, willpower struggled to master surrender—on both our parts.

When the music stopped and the dancers applauded the end of the *tanda*—four tangos danced in succession; we had only shared the last—he held me in the shadows edging the dance floor, his hand still at my back.

"You are an excellent dancer," he said, his voice low and edged with genuine kindness. Yet around the edges laced danger.

"As are you."

I stepped away from his possessive embrace, entering the air as if released from a hypnotic fog. I didn't turn to smile at him, or acknowledge that we'd just shared an incredible two minutes. Instead I walked toward the door and took the spiraling stone steps up to ground level.

I emerged on a touristy street in the fifth arrondissement. The night was bold with partying vacationers bouncing from club to club. Neon flashed in restaurant windows. Grilled, spiced lamb and fried cheese tinted the summer air. Shouts and chatter distracted passersby from noticing me, a woman flushed and breathing heavily, hand pressed to her chest.

I retrieved my backpack from the doorman, and slipped into the shadows of a narrow alleyway across the street.

Tonight the hunt had taken a turn. Soon my prey would relent.

In a hundred years, I, Alexandre Renard, have never met a more frustrating, yet intriguing woman.

I suppose she thought her dramatic exit from the tango club would leave me wanting more, actually render me to pine for the mysterious woman who followed my lead masterfully. Our first dance, even. Her body had been fine, pressed next to mine. Not too slender, curves in all the right places. She was a woman. A real woman.

A woman who I was aware had tracked me for a couple weeks. I cannot be sure if she has followed me since I arrived in Paris on a sort of getaway-to-take-stock-of-my-life excursion. It was unlikely, though, that she could have followed from my home state of Minnesota.

Did she think I was not aware? Silly girl. I've been waiting for her to make a move. When she met my eyes across the dance floor, I held her gaze. I don't know what color those eyes were, but I do know they were sad. So sad. Why?

I decided to sit out the next *tanda* of dances. Perhaps

I would leave for the night. Since arriving, this club has been a salvation to me. I came here, after a suggestion from my tribe leader, to forget things that will never completely leave my blood. Memories embedded within my very DNA.

For three minutes tonight, I forgot the painful snapshots from my past. It was lovely.

But I don't believe it's going to get any lovelier. Interesting, yes. Exciting? Highly likely. But like the tango, I sense the relationship I have begun with the woman with sad eyes will only grow more volatile.

I wager she's lurking outside, waiting in the shadows for me. It is her MO. I know what she wants—blood.

I am willing to play along to see how far she will go to get it.

CHAPTER TWO

SOMEHOW I MISSED Alexandre leaving the tango club last night. I don't know how that happened. Sure, the crowd was thick, but my attention veered from the club entrance only once or twice. I'm usually top of my game when it comes to tracking.

Considering I've only tracked the one mark, I'd say I'm doing well.

So the mark had slipped my radar. Fine. I had needed some breathing room after standing close to him, walking the dance floor with him in a suggestive clutch. I admit it. The guy had smoldered his sex appeal right into my skin.

I rubbed my bare arms now as I weaved through the dancers gathered in the dark shadows of the club. He showed here every night after eleven. Danced with two or three different women. Sometimes he left alone. Sometimes he left with a looker snuggled in his embrace.

What he did with those women was abominable.

I would stop him tonight. I had to, or I'd never be able to face what my future held.

A chirp of the bandoneón invited dancers onto the floor. I lingered near the brick wall for this dance. I wanted to sight my mark.

He moved around the floor with a blonde woman who was taller than he. He kept their embrace open, not committing to intimacy beyond the control of the dance. I liked that. If he was going to dance close with anyone tonight, it had better be me.

Well, er…strictly as a condition of the hunt, of course.

I stretched my right leg out, toward the dance floor. Tonight I wore a slim-fitting deep violet dress cut as low in the back as it was in the front. A few spangles occasionally caught the smoke-muted lights and glinted. It made me feel sexy. So little, lately, actually did.

He passed by me, and our gazes held for a moment longer than his partner preferred. She stretched her arm around behind his neck and touched him. He turned and scowled at her pleading pout.

With a simple twirl, he delivered his partner from the floor. A quick dismissal.

As the next song began, he walked up to me.

"Now that you are here," he said, leaning in so I could hear over the music, "I won't be able to concentrate."

Now if that wasn't a line…

He clasped my hand, tentatively sliding his other hand up my back. An invitation. He would not move until I gave him a subtle signal. I arched my back, snugging my chest against his. We'd gone beyond mutual distance; the closer the better. It gave me, the hunter, the advantage.

And he stepped back on his left foot to begin our duel.

We walked, he judging my moves and leading with that knowledge. He made following effortless, like taking a breath.

If only I could breathe like this forever.

A slide of my foot between his ankles drew him closer, and again we stood face-to-face. Our chests close, I could feel his heartbeat—a surprise—against mine. The pulse of his blood gushing through his veins pounded within me as if a seductive bass beat.

Our mouths close, I breathed in his cinnamon aura, and briefly, I imagined what it might be like to kiss him. All consuming, surely. I'd fall into his dark allure and never rise again, nor would I wish to. He'd seduce me with that kiss—and then the sharp reminder of his reality would cut me.

I broke the close embrace and performed a feint by kicking one foot across my other.

Chuckling lowly, he forced me closer and into a walk

that would see me depending on him for balance until he angled toward the center of the dance floor and straightened his posture.

His soft chuckle spilled over my exposed cleavage like a lover's kisses. I leaned into him and felt him arch backward. He drew me forward along his body. I surrendered, bending forward on one leg and leaning back, stretching out my other leg behind me. He mastered me with his fierce gaze as we held the pose.

"You're dangerous," I said.

"And you are teasing me," he replied as I stared up at him, completely at his command. "Slayer."

The music paused a beat. As did my heart. He knew? But how?

Returned to standing position, I twisted my hand within his clasp, but he wasn't about to release me from this dance. We walked more swiftly, hip-to-hip, facing forward, our path determined and insistent.

"How did you know?"

"I didn't. You've been following me for weeks," he said. "I made an assumption that you just confirmed."

Damn. "The game is over for the night."

He didn't answer, and I parted from him and walked off the floor, brushing aside the disheveled bangs from my lashes. I clutched a palm over my rapid heartbeats.

"This doesn't have to be a game," I heard him say over the music.

This time I did glance back. He stood with his hand held out, entreating. Daring me into his world. A dangerous dance of opposites.

Something inside me wanted to return to the seductive menace of his arms, but I couldn't face my failure. I turned and strode out, marking this night unsuccessful.

I gave her ten minutes before I left the club and moved through the tourist crowd without touching a soul. Mortals parted at my silent command, unaware their minds were being subtly manipulated.

I hadn't expected my dance partner to retreat. Perhaps she wasn't so bold as I'd initially thought. She'd looked hurt when I'd named her a slayer.

Hell, a vampire has to keep his eyes peeled for her kind.

But was she really that kind? I sensed she was rather new at the job. And proof came when I rounded the corner to find my sexy little slayer backed against the wall by two men who I knew were vampires.

A wooden stake lay on the ground by her black velvet high heels. The side of her dress was torn to the hip revealing the top of her thigh-high black stocking.

I charged and tore one vamp away from her. The other went for her neck, fangs bared. A punch to my gut did little more than anger me further. I fisted the vampire under the jaw. He staggered backward. Slipping around,

I grabbed his head with both hands and twisted sharply. The move would have killed a human. As the vampire slid in a heap before me, I knew he'd revive quickly.

The slayer screamed. I lunged for the stake and shoved it in the attacking vampire's back. Ash dispersed before me to reveal the wide, frightened eyes of my daring dancer.

I looked at the stake, dripping with blood—from my own kind. Abominable. I had never… I would be punished by my own for the crime. It was only just.

An angel lured me from the dire thought.

"You saved my life," she said on a nervous warble. She shook her head and smiled. Gripping my face between her hands, she stepped up and kissed me.

A nervous reaction to the adrenaline rush? Mercy, but her mouth was firm and lush and, when the few seconds required for a thank-you kiss had expired, she melted against my body more easily than she had when we'd tangoed.

And then she fainted in my arms.

CHAPTER THREE

FLOATING ON A DREAM of cinnamon-scented desire, I resurfaced with a moan and a sigh. Opening my eyes I looked up into the darkest, sexiest eyes I had ever looked into.

Damn, it was the vampire.

I shoved at him, but realized he held me draped in his arms. That made for an awkward tumble away from him and a landing that found me clutching for my front door-knob.

My door?

"How did you know where I live?"

He leaned against the door frame, suave and debonair in his pin-striped suit coat indicative of the Argentine tango. "You've been following me. I've been following you."

"Only on the dance floor, buddy."

"Do not lie to me, pretty slayer. Each night I sensed your presence as I left the club. Ever watching. I wondered how long it would take you to approach me. Never dreamed it would be on the dance floor."

"Yeah?" I shoved the key in the lock. "That was my mistake. I should have staked you the first night I saw you."

"Why didn't you?"

I walked inside the cool darkness of my living room, gesturing he follow. I was too tired to argue. Mad rushes of adrenaline had taken away my energy. I turned to find a smirking vampire inside the doorway, leaning against the wall.

Oh hell.

With a casual sweep of my hand, I'd given him permission to enter. Now he could enter freely whenever he chose. Had I learned nothing from my training over the past year?

"You haven't done this before, have you?"

He approached, and I had the forethought to whip out my stake, which, surprisingly, he must have retrieved and tucked in my purse.

"Stay back, vampire."

He walked right to the point of the stake and pressed his chest against the tip I had honed myself. I winced, but did not relent. He scanned the room, taking in the clutter stacked on the rosewood secretary to my side, the chaise longue drowning in velvet pillows, and down the hallway where my bedroom door hung open.

He grasped the stake and held it firmly at his chest. "What is your name?"

"Ver—Veronica Marshall."

"Veronica," he repeated, yet he made the name sound sexier than I'd ever felt it sounded. "I'm giving you a freebie here, Veronica. Why won't you do it?"

"I...don't know." I clasped the stake. Furrowed my brow. "It's not supposed to be like this. You're supposed to growl at me and flash your fangs."

"Like the vamps in the alley? They could have killed you."

"I know." I tugged the stake from his grip and tossed it over my shoulder.

What I next did is difficult to explain beyond that my heart insisted I follow this particular dance step.

I pressed my face against his shoulder and my palms to his chest. Seeking safety. A slayer snuggling up to a vampire? That was wrong in so many ways.

"You were to be my first," I whispered, clinging to him. Just wanting rescue. Someone who would lead, so I could follow. "I know I can do it—stake a vampire. But, not yet. I...need time."

"And you expect me to wait around for you to muster up the courage?"

"No."

"You only get one freebie."

"I know, I— Alexandre, why did you save me? Have you ever killed another vampire like that?"

Head bowed, he didn't meet my eyes. "A man can be forced to do terrible things. I will be hunted for the crime of killing one of my own. Doesn't matter. I had to protect you."

"No, you didn't have to. It wasn't force. I'm a slayer. Your enemy!"

"Yes." He tilted my head up and brushed his thumb over my mouth. "I had to do it, or we would have never danced again."

Inhaling, I stepped closer to him, and he clasped my hand, drawing us into a snug tango embrace. We stepped minutely, our faces tilted into one another. His breath stealing mine. Our chests crushed together. My thigh caressed his.

"Kiss me," I said.

When a woman asks a man for a kiss, no fool would refuse. I was not that fool. Even if it did disturb me I was kissing the woman who had just held a stake to my heart. She seemed determined to accomplish her deadly task. Just…not right now.

I could deal with that.

Though we'd stopped moving in a dance embrace, we were still performing the tango. I savored the tango's dance of emotions between love and hate, joy and pain, even the middle ground of like and disinterest.

Veronica's mouth had been made to fit mine. I could not get enough of her taste, her soft sighing moans, that supple body rubbing against mine.

I pushed her against the wall, drawing my hands up her arms and pinning her wrists gently above her head. I could not resist the need to own her, to show her I could take control at any moment, no matter the danger she presented.

She twined her leg along mine, drawing the hard toe of her high heel up my shin. My fingers played across the silken black stocking that had been revealed by the rip in her dress.

Mercy. It had been too long since a woman had blasted my discretion to hell. Had made me want her despite the ridiculous clash of our natures. We were not meant to share such an embrace.

Only fools tempted the devil Himself. I made a point of avoiding that dark prince. Yet I suspected he would get a chuckle at our expense.

I slid the sleeve from Veronica's shoulder, and marked the newly exposed skin with kisses. So soft there, scented with cherries and vanilla. My fangs descended, wanting their due, so I closed my mouth to prevent cutting her flesh.

My dangerous dancer arched toward me. Silently she said, "It's okay, continue."

And when I moved my mouth across the soft mound of her breast, she tilted back her head. I dashed my tongue behind the dress and licked her nipple. Her moan accompanied a deft move as she hooked her ankle behind my calf, anchoring herself to me.

Be damned wicked memories, I could not leave her alone tonight. The moon was still high in the sky. It would not be daylight for hours.

I swept Veronica into my arms. Without a word, our gazes agreed. This embrace would not end.

CHAPTER FOUR

MOONLIGHT PERMEATED the thin white sheers in my bedroom. I don't like sleeping in complete darkness. The cold light found my lover's skin and dazzled upon it. I slipped off Alexandre's shirt and let it drop as we walked—me backward—toward the bed. This dance step excited me and at the same time made me anxious.

A vampire stood in my bedroom. A vampire kissed my neck. His fingers glided over the shoulders of my dress, shoving down the spangled fabric. His mouth followed the path of his fingers, moving those dangerous fangs away from my neck.

A relief. Yet I knew a vampire could bite a person anywhere. Blood shimmied through my veins, warming and flushing my skin. But would it excite him a little too much?

Distracting myself from the unknown, I ran my palms down his bare chest. "You are so beautiful." The hard ridges of his muscles pulsed.

"Men are not beautiful," he whispered against my breast. He moved my arm back, which was all it took to allow the dress to slide from my breasts, over my hips, and to the floor. "Only women can touch beauty. And you are a goddess, Veronica."

"I mean you're a wondrous thing to look at." Scooching up onto the bed, I tugged him to me and bracketed his hips with my knees. I wore but the silk thigh stockings. "Do you work out?"

"As you have seen, I dance."

"Dancing does not do this." I swept another appreciative palm over his rigid abs. "How long have you danced?"

He dipped his head to my breast and tongued my nipple. Hot and firm, his tongue flicked rapidly, making me squirm and I couldn't stop a moan.

"Decades," he murmured. "It takes me away from the world. I can think of nothing but the movement when I dance. How long have you danced?"

"My father taught me when I was young." I bowed my head to the top of his and closed my eyes, shuddering as his attentions stirred the core of me. "We dance for the same reason—to be taken away."

"I can take you away now." He licked down my stom-

ach, cupping both my breasts. "Spread your legs, Veronica. Let me kiss you there."

My fingers slipped through his hair, grasping and
wondering if I should stop his explorations. Always that
nervous twitter when a man kisses you so intimately. But
the first strike of his tongue between my legs branded
me.

I was his. This not-so-expert slayer was making love
with her prey. And it wasn't a trick to lure him into a
trap.

Or maybe this was his trick, to lull me into a state of
ignorant bliss. And then…he would pierce me with his
fangs and destroy me.

My life was already marked for early expiration. If I
was going to go, I choose the vampire's bite. Please. And
make it slow, painful and so, so delicious.

Sex and biting go hand in hand. I rarely enjoyed one
without the other. When I did bite without considering
sex it was usually a quick, necessary extraction from a
random person in a dark alley. Sex with strangers can get
tedious if you have to persuade them to forget the bite
before sending them on their way home.

I had no intention of enthralling Veronica's mind. It
would be a lie. A wicked manipulation she did not deserve. I cared too much for her. Though we had only
been in contact a few days, I'd thought about her every

waking moment in the preceding weeks when she'd been tracking me.

I was already in love with her accidental bravery, her misplaced daring. Her desperate desire to make a kill to prove—well, what, I wasn't sure. She was no slayer, yet I felt this kill would prove symbolic to her somehow.

To steal her lifeblood now would be a cruel victory. I didn't need it. I wanted to taste Veronica's blood, but it could wait. Tonight, was for sealing us in an unbreakable hold no dancer could resist.

I willed my fangs up so I would not risk cutting her flesh. Once I tasted blood, I would not be so in control of my dark hungers.

She moaned sweetly at my command. Her body slicked beneath my tongue as I tasted every inch of skin seasoned with cherries, vanilla, salt and a hint of smoke from the *milonga*. I devoured every undulating muscle the tango had honed, and every soft curve dancing could not steal from her femininity.

I felt her trace the scar that ran from the side of my neck and around back. "I didn't think a vampire could scar. What's it from?"

"Not a good memory."

"You'd rather not talk about it?"

"Not now, Veronica. Only us tonight…nothing dismal. Mmm…" I traced my tongue along her thigh. Her stomach was soft, rounded, so sweet.

"You won't…" she suddenly said, as I kissed beneath her breast.

I knew what she dared not ask. "No, lover. Not tonight." I dashed my tongue beneath my upper teeth. Fangs were up. "Does that make you more comfortable?"

Her chest sank as she exhaled. Relief.

Disappointment caused me to pause, my cheek aside her breast. She had accepted me into her bed, but I would ever be a monster to those unlike me.

Yet we monsters were endlessly fascinated by others.

Her fingers tickled through my hair and I smiled against her flesh. "Come here," she said.

Gliding up alongside her, I moaned as she slid a hand inside my trousers. I flicked open the fly and kicked the pants off my legs.

"So hard," she whispered aside my ear, as her fingers explored me. "And thick. I'm not sure…"

"We will fit," I reassured, but took the surprise in her tone as a compliment. "We were made to dance with one another, Veronica."

Her leg wrapped around behind my hips, and I slid to press my erection against her mons. Already I shuddered with imminent release. The intimate shape of our hold could be duplicated on the dance floor, she following my lead, her hand about my neck to confirm or deny what I asked of her.

With one roll of my torso, I entered her slowly, gauging her whimpers and gasps so I would not be too rough. I became the follower, taking her lead. A tango beat pulsed in my blood, daring me further.

Slowly, ever deeper, I found the core of her. Hugged so tightly I had barely to move. Our breathing, heavy and frantic, strummed muscles and played her inner walls, clasping, holding, winning.

I cried out and stiffened above her. Fingernails raked my chest, gouging sweet pain in the wake of delicious triumph. And as my climax fluttered away Veronica's body arched up toward me, and she tumbled over the edge. The intensity of her surrender stole me into her realm.

I wished to never leave.

"Veronica," I whispered, and kissed her mouth. My fangs had descended again and I grazed them along her jaw. "You have claimed me."

CHAPTER FIVE

WAKING ABRUPTLY, I slid off the bed, my bare feet landing on the cool ceramic tile. I always come awake ready to hit the pavement. Caffeine has never been a part of my lexicon.

I glanced to the bed. He lay so still. His gorgeous body was visible now that my eyes adjusted to the darkness. Arms folded above his head on the pillow, his length stretched at an angle across the mattress. No sheet covered him. The temptation to glide my fingers down the hard plane of his stomach and touch the now-soft part of him that had impaled me earlier twitched my fingers.

Indeed, we had fit together perfectly, even despite my apprehensions. I'd never experienced lovemaking like that before. So intense, the man utterly focused on my needs. And to feel him climax within me had been amazing.

It was an exquisite going away present—for both of us.

Tiptoeing through the shadows drawn across the floor by the slatted blinds, I glanced to the clock: 4:00 a.m. The sun wasn't due for a few hours. I had plenty of time.

But Alexandre did not.

Out in the living room, the wooden stake lay on the floor by my backpack. It was solid in my grip. A real weapon I had been trained to use. And this vampire did not intimidate me as those two in the alley had.

Finally I would have closure. A girl couldn't say good-bye without putting a few things in order, and I had a strange desire to not leave this world without a farewell. I needed to do some good first.

Back in the bedroom, I stood over the bed listening for signs of life, a quiet snore. Alexandre breathed, but he lay still, as if marble. It was creepy until I glided my eyes down his gorgeous torso. Those buff abs and solid-as-rock muscles—no. I'd done admiration.

This man was a vampire. He had…immortality. Something I could never touch. That was not fair.

Breaths racing, I raised the stake above my head with both hands. I leaned forward, preparing to plunge it through flesh and muscle to burst the heart.

If he were to suddenly open his eyes and look right at me, it would devastate me. Like a scene from some horror movie gone bad. But he didn't. The vampire wasn't aware death loomed over him.

My fingers twisted around the wood, tightening. Sweat warmed my grasp. I closed my eyes.

"Goodbye," I whispered, and lunged—my swing backward, away from the bed. I tossed the stake aside and ran from the room.

Vampires need little sleep. I usually only drift off after great sex. So it didn't surprise me to wake in a strange bed. The lingering scent of Veronica's perfume calmed any rising apprehensions.

What did surprise me was the wooden stake lying next to my hip. I startled upright and grabbed the thing, wielding it as if to stab. Veronica wasn't in the room, but she must have been here.

Had she been going to stake me?

I swiped a hand down my face and swung my legs over the side of the bed. My trousers were close and I pulled them on. I zipped and buttoned them, but didn't bother with my shirt.

A glance out the window showed me that I had about an hour to get home before the sun rose. I could do sunlight in small increments. It wasn't as though when I stepped into sun I'd burst into flames. But I did burn, quickly.

Crying led me into the living room. She sat near the

floor-to-ceiling window, her head against the glass. Tears spattered the glass like raindrops.

I squatted next to her, but felt words were inappropriate. I displayed the stake before her. She grabbed it from me and threw it across the room. It clattered against the opposite wall.

"I was going to kill you. All right?" she said on huffing breaths. "Don't you hate me?"

"But you did not."

"I couldn't. I…I think I really care about you."

Taken aback at that confession, both of us.

"And besides, I can't do this," she said, her lip trembling. "It was supposed to make me feel better. To allow me to reclaim my control before it was lost. And I was supposed to do something good for others before I… well… But staking you? No, that's not good. You're no threat. And I am not a killer."

"Something good?" She made some sense, but she was rambling in a frantic emotional tirade. She hid something from me. I'd sensed it as we'd danced. She was too tense, not completely prepared to surrender. "Why do you have to do something good before…?"

She nestled her head to my chest and I dragged her onto my lap. Leaning against the window I held her, naked and warm. I wanted to kiss her, to stroke her soft skin, and begin making love again. But I would not toy with the obvious pain I sensed she felt.

"I'm dying," she said softly. Now the tears had stopped. She spoke plainly but slowly. "Huntington's disease. Soon it'll affect my dancing because it attacks the muscles, and it kills very quickly following that. There's no cure."

I hugged her tightly, not wanting to give her up to anything unseen or visible. The world could be very cruel to mortals.

"For a year I've been training to be a slayer. A man approached me after a support group meeting. He told me about vampires, and proved to me they exist. He said I could do a good thing by exterminating them. That they harmed mortals. And…it was a means to kill that which I couldn't have."

"Eternity," I said.

My heart sunk in my chest. I understood nothing about fatal diseases. But with modern medicine could they not cure everything? Why had this gorgeous woman been chosen for an early death? Didn't seem fair.

And yet another woman I had known had been chosen for the same fate. That hadn't been fair, either.

I clenched a fist against Veronica's stomach. Despite best intentions to forget everything, my past had just walked back into my life.

She lifted her head and stared into my eyes. "Alexandre, you changed me. Dancing with you. Making love. You're so giving. You're not a monster."

"I try not to be."

"I was only taught vampires are monsters. Some slayer I turned out to be, eh?"

"The stake lies a few feet away."

"Forget the stake. I've been told I have a year to live. If I could dance every day with you, that would make dying easier."

"No, please, you cannot…" I couldn't say it. I would not. She needed strength. "I will be waiting for you on the dance floor every night, Veronica. Promise."

CHAPTER SIX

WHAT HAD I done wrong? This man was supposed to be my enemy. An enemy to mortals who walked the streets, warm blood gushing through their veins. Yet he hadn't bitten me, despite the fact I knew his fangs had been down when we'd made love.

If he did bite me, could he give me the eternity my disease would steal from me?

I couldn't think like that. No mortal had eternity. And I didn't want what the vampire had.

Or did I?

"I would offer to change your future," Alexandre whispered.

He stroked a curl of hair from my cheek. The attention was so personal, so genuine. He wanted to be here, and I couldn't imagine him giving anyone else such intense consideration.

"But I would not wish the life I have on anyone. Life is what you are given. To change you would be—"

"Cheating," I finished. "I don't want to be a vampire, Alexandre. I don't think. You…didn't bite me last night when we were making love. Is it because you had no desire to?"

"Veronica, I desire everything about you. Your lips, your body, your sweet, strained moans—and your blood. But I don't need to drink more than once a week. I wanted you to feel safe with me, because you are."

"But isn't it a sex thing? I was taught sex and biting go hand in hand with vampires."

"Most of the time, yes, but not always. And when I don't bite you, yet make love to your entire body, it is so delicious. My focus is only on you, not on fulfilling my wants."

"That was some damn good sex." I turned in his embrace and put my bare feet on the window.

Completely naked, I was comfortable melting against him. So much had been taken from me with my diagnosis. I'd didn't worry about the "living every moment to the hilt" thing so much as I mourned never having had a fulfilling and loving relationship with a man.

The disease made me feel unlovable, unattractive and disposable. Yet sitting here in Alexandre's embrace I'd never felt so alive and noticed before. I arched my back, lifting my breasts, because I felt sexy, and it was an amazing release of my inhibitions.

"Do you need to leave soon?" I wondered.

"Yes." He caressed my breast and kissed my shoulder. "But let's talk until I must rush away from you. I like holding you like this. Is...your condition inherited? Or was it something you caught?"

"Inherited. From my mother's side. She didn't die that way, though. My parents were killed in a car crash. What about you? Your condition?"

His chuckle rumbled in his chest. It permeated my body and tickled my insides. Sliding my toes along his pants leg, I nestled tight against his chest.

"I didn't ask for vampirism," he said. "In fact, it was forced on me."

"Tell me about it?"

"I..."

"If it's a bad memory you don't have to."

"I will tell you because you are the first woman in a long time I feel connected to. Safe."

"Seriously? With a stake not far away?"

"Yes, even with that damned stake in eye's view."

"I was married at the turn of last century," I began.

Veronica sat on my lap, the two of us facing the gray sky, which had begun to lighten with the threat of daylight. I didn't worry about escaping. I didn't want to leave

Veronica now knowing how short the days could actually be between us.

"I loved my wife, Maria. But I had to leave her during the day to work the coal mines. We lived in the Yosemite Valley at the end of the nineteenth century. Little mining town I'd grown up in. One evening I returned to find the door off its hinges. I rushed inside and found Maria sitting on the floor, her dress tattered, blood on her hands and face and a dagger stuck in her heart."

I felt Veronica tense on my lap. Her heartbeats raced mine.

"Maria whispered 'I love you,' and then she died. Thieves had claimed the gold locket from around her neck. She had been raped, and left to die. I realized later, she had sat there for hours with the dagger in her heart, hanging on, waiting for my return. And when finally she saw me, she was able to stop her struggle to survive.

"I went on a rampage. I knew exactly who had done it—the Crow gang. Three brothers who drank, stole and tormented all the women in the town. I killed all three of them, and another man who merely got in my way."

"I was sentenced to hang three days following. For avenging my wife's death. I didn't care. Be damned to them all. I could not live without Maria. I went to my death willingly."

Veronica clutched my tight fists and kissed them ten-

derly. Her warm teardrops stained my flesh and I remembered Maria's warm blood seeping into my skin.

I swallowed the desire to shout until my lungs ached,
and hugged Veronica desperately.

"I was hanged at midnight. But the rope did not snap
my neck, and I struggled, fighting the noose, wishing I
would simply die. The crowd left when they thought I
was surely dead for I'd stopped kicking. But yet I sensed
the world.

"When the moon was high in the sky the vampire arrived and cut me down. He bit into my neck, smirked and
pronounced me strong and vital. It wasn't my time to die
yet. He dumped me in his wagon and sought the darkness of an abandoned mining cave. After my strength
returned, I fought him. He was stronger. Life without
Maria was unimaginable. I tried to kill myself by slitting
my wrists. But I was already vampire. And so there you
have it."

"You eventually decided to live."

"Yes, I accepted what life had given me. It took me a
long time to get over Maria's death. Some days I'm still
not over it. Hence my visit to Paris. I thought I could
chase away the memory. I have moved on, but the memories stick into my bones as if they were metal spikes."

"Thank you for telling me that, Alexandre. I'm so
sorry about your wife."

I kissed the crown of Veronica's head. "So am I. No one will replace her."

"I imagine not. The scar on your neck…"

"From the hangman's noose."

She sighed, but then jerked in my embrace. "Oh my God, the sun is on the horizon."

"I can slip along the shadows of the buildings to get home. Will I see you on the dance floor tonight?"

"I'll be there."

CHAPTER SEVEN

MY ATTEMPT to become a heartless assassin had failed. Thankfully. I was no killer. That I'd gone through the motions, and gained confidence and learned how to act and react in a dangerous situation had shattered my desire for witless revenge against something I could never stop.

No one wants to die. But I wasn't angry about it anymore. Death isn't spiteful. It doesn't pick and choose. It is random. So random as to steal an innocent woman from her loving husband and then force him to witness her pain.

Oh, Alexandre. How he must have suffered to know he would live forever yet could never give that life to Maria. I am glad he chose life, and hadn't become reckless and attempted to make someone stake him.

I didn't need immortality. Nor did I want to replace Maria. I wouldn't be around long enough to matter to him. But I did want all the time with Alexandre I could manage.

I dressed in my sexiest dress tonight. It was sheer red with discreet lining, yet when the light hit it just so, it made me look as if I was nude beneath.

As usual the dress plunged in the back. I loved the feel of Alexandre's hand against my flesh as we danced. He never tried to force me into a move. He was the consummate leader in that he suggested the direction he'd like to go, but if I desired a different path, then he followed.

Exactly how he was off the dance floor.

How could a vampire be so caring? They couldn't all be monsters. Why had I never questioned my training once? My teacher had been most convincing they were all evil.

I sniffed away a tear thinking of Alexandre walking in to find his wife who had tendered her last breaths until he returned home to finally die. And now he had to live with that pain an eternity. Forever. It wasn't as though a person could erase memory.

Truly, immortality was not all it was cracked up to be.

I wanted to make his eternity more bearable. If he would allow it.

Locking the door and skipping down the steps, I made the dance club quickly and pushed through the crowd.

My lover stood at the edge of the dance floor, his hand held out for me to clasp.

We danced the first *tanda*, and the second without pause. Eight tangos. Eight heart-racing moments of passion-laced contact. Eight more sweet memories to carry with me the rest of my days.

I was determined to dance until sunrise with Veronica.

After pausing to sip some water (she doesn't like alcohol and I find it goes to my head too quickly) we resumed the dimly lit dance floor. We refused the open embrace. Why the distance when we could press close and talk to one another without speaking a word?

When a man leads the tango his intentions come from his chest and torso. Veronica read my intent as if she were the interpreter of my unique language. We walked counterclockwise around the circumference of the floor, avoiding the poseurs who occupied the middle.

When I signaled my intention, she paused minutely, and I knew she preferred a switch to lead. I allowed it because following her is daring and yet submissive, but also, it made me feel so strong I surrendered willingly.

After a dozen or so dances, I had fallen into the bliss our connection forged. The music provided but a setting to our private embrace. No one else mattered.

I nudged aside a wisp of dark hair from her cheek, and whispered at Veronica's ear, "I love you."

Her body reacted. Her breasts hugging at my chest, I felt her hard nipples through my shirt. She slid her leg along mine, drawing it up and caressing my shin with her toe. Sexual conversation via a dance move.

We held there for a few beats, unmindful of the dancers moving around us. We committed a faux pas by pausing too long and forcing others to bypass us. Neither of us cared.

"I love you, too," she said at my mouth.

I tasted her words and kissed her quickly. We twisted and stepped backward. No time to pause for a longer kiss. That short contact was more perfect than any other. For it sealed a pact between the two of us—slayer and vampire.

"Let's go home and make love," I said to her.

"I thought we already were."

"We are. But I prefer the dance move that sees you naked and pressed against me."

"Will you bite me, Alexandre?"

I broke the embrace and studied her eyes. No wonder, no teasing. She was serious.

"Just a bite," I said. "Nothing more." Meaning, we would not make her a vampire. She wasn't ready for it. I was, perhaps.

No. I would not go there. Could not dream…

"Right. Just that." She wanted something different. Something she could never completely understand. A dark tease at immortality. A sacrifice of soul. "I want you to have a part of me. So you'll never forget me."

I looked aside. I didn't want her to see the tear welling at the corner of my eye.

I had been transformed to vampire against my will. I would never do that to someone. Yet hadn't Veronica the right to ask for the life she should be granted? Who was I to determine the right and wrong of it?

My world was horrible, dangerous, the battle we vampires had with the werewolves keep me vigilant. And yet my world was also remarkable, forgiving and promised an endless future.

I could not decide what was more deplorable—Veronica's sentence or mine.

CHAPTER EIGHT

WE SURFACED from the dance club to chaos. A fire engine was parked before the adjacent building, and flames whipped out of the building's windows.

Alexandre pushed me left, away from the havoc, yet he veered right. I let him go. He spoke to one of the firemen, nodding and pointing to the building. He wanted to make sure everyone was all right, that no one had been trapped inside.

How many bloodsucking vampires would have the same concern for mere humans?

Flushed with admiration for him, I leaned against something solid and smiled to myself. And then the solid thing locked its arms about me.

I got half a scream out before he clamped a hand over my mouth and dragged me down the street. Arms flailing, I groped for hold on anything, a chair placed before a restaurant, the railing of a gate before that same restaurant. I kicked backward, but he was too strong.

And he was a vampire—because he reeked of blood.

When we arrived at a T where the road turned left and right down an alley, he stopped and took his hand from my mouth. I screamed Alexandre's name, but realized too late, that was what my captor had wanted.

Alexandre turned, scanning where he had left me. He tracked down the street. When his sight pinpointed me, the vampire whisked me to the right, and handed me over to another burly man who waited. He bent and hefted me over his shoulder, and took off running.

They would lead my lover into a trap.

Whether or not it was I who wielded the stake, I would be the death of Alexandre.

The fire had been a cruel distraction. I knew it as my heart pounded viciously against my rib cage.

This would be my punishment for killing one of my own.

I stroked my fingers over the scar running along my neck. Not if I had anything to say about it.

Vampirism grants me supernatural speed. I turned the corner into the alleyway but seconds after I'd heard Veronica scream. Unfortunately vampirism made her captors quick, too. Two blocks ahead, they disappeared to the left.

Passing an iron gate that decorated the front of a tourist shop, I grabbed the iron post and bent it, twisting to break it off. A makeshift stake. I would kill them all if they harmed one centimeter of her flesh.

It was happening again. Another senseless crime against my heart.

It had been a long time since I had allowed myself to feel anything for a woman beyond friendship or to use her as a sex partner. I cared for Veronica. I could even admit I loved her. Dancing together had quickened our intimacy, and I had probably known that first dance she was the one woman I had been searching for since Maria's murder.

"Not again," I growled. "They won't take the woman I love away from me."

I smashed the iron bar across the corner of a brick building as I rounded it swiftly. My fangs lowered. I would tear out hearts if I had to.

There, beyond an open iron gate, a garden was tucked between two buildings. It was common in the city to find these secret alcoves. The heady scent of some flower I couldn't name overwhelmed the cherry and vanilla scent I had followed. Veronica's scream routed through my senses and opened my pores to her innate fragrance. It was flooded with fear, an acrid odor I could literally taste.

Slipping by the low-hanging vines dusted heavy flower blooms across my shoulder. I walked into the depths of the garden. There at the far wall laced with more wild vines, held by two vampires, stood Veronica. She didn't struggle; she looked ready to pass out.

Before them stood Bruce Westing, a lackey for the Anakim tribe, who had tried to convince me to join them upon arrival in Paris. I already belonged to tribe Nava back in the States. Vampires could switch alliances at will, but I was not interested in a tribe of vampires who believed they had descended from bloodsucking giants.

I held the iron stake near my hip, my knuckles tight.

"You killed one of our own?" Bruce tossed out in mocking disbelief. "Alexandre, have we not walked a wide path around one another as agreed? You do your thing, we do ours?"

"They were going to kill her," I said. It was the wrong thing to say.

"She was going to slay them!"

"Oh, come on. Her?" I wanted to meet Veronica's eyes, to convey I was going to get her out of this some-how, but it was wiser to focus on Bruce. "She's a bitty thing. The moment your men were on her she lost all confidence. She couldn't slay a mouse."

I did catch Veronica's defiant *hmmph*. I loved her for her spunk.

I loved her for her daring.

I loved her for the silent language we spoke when we danced.

"Let her go," I said. "You'll gain no favor by taking out an innocent."

"Whether she possesses any ability to slay or just likes to blow smoke," Bruce said, "she is a slayer. If you hadn't been fucking her, you'd have taken her out by now, too."

"Enough!" Lowering my head, but keeping my eyes on Bruce, I growled deeply, showing my fangs. "Release her."

"You'll have to stake me to get to her," he offered, spreading his arms to display his chest as a target. His fangs were exposed in challenge as well. "But I promise my men can break her pretty little neck before I pluck that pitiful stake you're holding from my chest."

"It will kill you." I spun the iron stake between my fingers.

The argument was futile. I could stake the man, but indeed, Veronica would die while I was occupied with murder.

A new tactic was required.

I met Veronica's eyes. She shook her head subtly. Silly girl, she thought to influence my decision? She may have little time left on this earth, but I intended to ensure she enjoy every single one of those moments.

"Me for her," I said. "Release her and you can have me."

Bruce scratched the back of his head. "Yeah, I don't think so. I like spilling pretty girls' blood. And I really love it when they scream."

"She is dying," I argued. "It is some mortal cancer. She has but a few months left. You're not going to steal anything from her that hasn't already been taken away."

Bruce turned to Veronica. "Is that true?"

Veronica winced. If she dared to lie...

Bruce stalked up to her and slapped his hand to her cheek. I tensed.

"Tell me the truth," he said, using, I knew, subtle persuasion to influence her mind.

"I am," Veronica answered.

With a nod of his head, Bruce had his men release Veronica. "Take him."

"Wait!" I shouted.

"Now what?" Bruce asked dryly.

"Allow me to kiss her goodbye." I tossed the iron stake through the air and Bruce caught it smartly. "And then I am yours."

CHAPTER NINE

THE IDIOT VAMPS agreed to Alexandre's request. Now he would whisk me away from a sure massacre. Except, I knew the whisking away wasn't going to happen as Alexandre approached and his sad eyes told me everything I didn't want to see.

He was serious about surrendering himself to save me. *Me.* A woman who had but a year to live!

"Don't do this," I whispered as he neared me. My body shook palpably. My throat was dry. I couldn't calm myself. "After they kill you," I said quietly as he pressed his chest to mine as if to dance, "they'll come after me."

"You will run as soon as we've parted. I'll occupy them long enough to give you a head start. Kiss me, Veronica."

His mouth pressed to mine. Tears rolled down my

cheeks and wetted our lips. It was horrible. Bittersweet. Agonizing. I couldn't let him go—would not. Not ever.

"Allow me the kiss that will grant you freedom?" he whispered.

I knew what he asked. And I didn't have to consider the options I'd vacillated previously. "Yes," I simply said. "Bite me."

With his back to the waiting vampires, Alexandre bent into my neck. The intrusion of his fangs hurt but I did not cry out. He penetrated my flesh and the growl of satisfaction that accompanied shimmied throughout my being. He sucked hard, drawing out my blood. I felt no pleasure, could not.

This was our goodbye kiss.

Working too quickly for what I had hoped could have been a leisurely indulgence in one another's flesh, I took enough blood from Veronica to remember her taste, but not enough to satisfy the craving that had burned in me for days. I couldn't risk Bruce and his men suspecting.

Drawing out my teeth before she would experience the blissful orgasm that accompanied the vampire's kiss, I regretted not being able to grant her that pleasure.

"Run now, and think of me often." I shoved her away and turned to face Bruce. "Promise me she will be safe."

Bruce shrugged. Then he straightened and his gaze fixed to my face, intensely interested in something on it.

I thrust out my tongue to taste my flesh. Damn. A dribble of blood sat at the corner of my mouth.

The plan had changed.

"Run, Veronica!"

She paused, regret flashing in her bright eyes, then turned and took off. One of Bruce's thugs raced after her, but I met him with my arm straight out, catching him across the neck and clotheslining him flat onto his back.

Bruce charged me with the iron stake. I ducked and the iron bar rattled across the cobblestoned street.

The other thug jumped onto my back. He clenched his fingers about my throat. Obviously he was unaware I'd done the choking thing before, and had survived it even when human. I would not go down easily.

Spinning, I slammed backward against the brick wall, which succeeded in peeling the vamp from my shoulders.

My skull snapped upon my spine as Bruce's fist connected under my jaw. I groped for hold, to not collide into Bruce's body and my fingers landed a wooden stake tucked inside his jacket.

So that's how they would dispose of one of their own? I hadn't a right to argue seeing I'd used the same method.

Swinging out with the stake, I lashed around and the point found a soft landing in the back of the thug I'd tossed against the wall. Blood spattered my face.

Bruce ripped me away and flung me across the alley

to land the opposite wall. Vines tore and I shoved them from my arms. I'd dropped the stake.

Veronica stood in my peripheral view.

"No!" I shouted at her. "Get away from here!"

Bruce collided with me, wrenching my arm around behind my hip. We could go at this physical fighting all night. Unless one of us wielded a stake, punches and nose-smashes would get us nowhere.

Veronica's heels clicked closer. What was she doing?

The vampire I'd initially tossed to the ground shook his head and rose to his feet.

Veronica lunged to the ground, grabbed the stake— the vampire grabbed her by the hair.

I wrestled with Bruce, but the idiot was like a tic. In fact, he dug his fangs in at the back of my neck. I shouted and growled and twisted my head. My flesh tore but it was better than having some asshole's fangs in your skin.

Veronica screamed. I turned to see the vampire jerk her around by her hair. Her body twisted, and her hands swung up. The stake found its mark in her aggressor's chest. Blood sputtered out at the connection. The vamp thug ashed all over Veronica.

"Shit!" Realizing he was outnumbered, Bruce shoved off me. He spat blood at Veronica.

She wielded the stake boldly, her jaw tight and her expression don't-fuck-with-me. Vampire ash powdered her arms.

"Leave us," I demanded.

"You're marked, Renard," Bruce said sharply. "You want to protect a slayer? Then you've got the whole Anakim tribe after you, I promise that."

Again he spat blood. Hissing at Veronica, Bruce then marched off.

I rushed to Veronica, but she didn't soften into my embrace. She held the stake so tightly I thought she'd become frozen in the defiant pose.

"You're safe now," I told her. "You did it. You staked a vampire."

Her eyes fluttered, and she threw the stake away as if it had burned her. A frantic brushing wiped the ash from her arms. "Alexandre?"

I touched her neck where I'd left the bite unsealed by my saliva. There was still time. "Let me kiss your neck again. If I lick it and seal the wound with my saliva, then you won't become vampire."

"No." She slapped a hand to my chest to stop my advance.

Our eyes danced the push-pull duel of the tango. What did she ask? And did I have a right to refuse her?

"I want this," she finally said. "I want you. Forever."

EPILOGUE

IT'S BEEN A YEAR, and I have not returned to my doctor. He would either confirm I had but a day or week or month to live, or look at my test results with shock and proclaim me completely cured—and what was up with my blood? It wasn't…right.

I couldn't risk a lab technician studying my blood under a microscope.

Either result mattered little to me. I felt healthy. I choose not to think about what can kill me, but rather, what is worth living for.

Alexandre suspects my Huntington's was tackled when I became completely vampire. I am inclined to agree.

I stole life when I should have died. It was selfish.

It was a decision I will never regret.

Lying nestled to my lover's body, our skin breathing from each other, our fangs grazed veins. Biting another vampire and drinking his blood is orgasmic. We rarely take from mortals now. It isn't necessary when we have one another.

I may live for centuries. I may walk out the door tomorrow and be staked by a slayer seeking revenge for the cruelties life has served her. Each day is special to me. Each day I wake in my lover's arms.

Veronica and I returned to Minnesota immediately after our run-in with Anakim's nasties in Paris. She enjoys the cold winter, and I can't argue the sunless days are a boon for our kind.

I've resumed my work with the Rescue Project my tribe leader Creed Saint-Pierre assigned me. We rescue vampires captured by werewolves for the blood sport. It is fulfilling work to save one vampire from the cruelties of UV sickness—brought on by extreme and forced exposure to ultraviolet light—and imprisonment.

Returning home each morning to Veronica makes it all worth it.

I will never forget Maria, but now I've a new reason for my heart to beat.

We stood side by side now, adjusting clothing. Veronica curled a thin slice of her dark hair forward onto her cheek. The mirror reflected happiness. It will not always be so. Love is giddy and wonderful and dangerous and painful.

"Wouldn't have it any other way."

"What?" Veronica said, looking at me in the mirror.

"Us," I said. "You ready?"

I swung her into a tango embrace and dipped her back, bending low as she stretched out her body. I held her easily with one arm as I glided my other hand along her thigh and up to her breast.

"That's not a tango move, lover."

"Neither is this."

Swinging her to her feet, I caught her across the back and bowed to sink my fangs into her vein below her jaw. The sweet darkness of her spilled into my mouth.

This dance will give us forever.

* * * * *

A NIGHT WITH
A VAMPIRE

Cynthia Cooke

CHAPTER ONE

THE sky erupted in an explosion of red and orange hues hastening the day's end. Soon the vampires would be rising. Damn, she'd better hurry.

Xana pulled to a stop along the shoulder of the two-lane highway that wound through northern Califor-nia's coastal mountain range and killed the engine. She popped open the glove box and slipped out her Glock. She hurriedly placed it inside her waistband against the small of her back and then grabbed two thin wooden stakes sharpened to needle-fine points and placed one in each of her back pockets.

She snatched her brother's—Cayman's—pack off the floor then climbed out of her truck, tucking her hands into her leather jacket pockets, cupping the five-point silver stars in each palm as she started down the mountain path.

Below her the valley twinkled in a sea of lights, but up here, she was alone. Isolated. She took a deep eucalyptus-scented breath as the wind picked up and listened for Cayman beyond the rustling of the leaves. Nothing. She kept to the path heading toward a warehouse. Why would Cayman have come here without her? He knew better, and it pissed her off. But lately he'd been hiding something, keeping secrets and pulling dumb stunts.

Like this one.

A pulse of electricity zapped the hair on the back of her neck and sent a shiver across her shoulders. She glanced behind her, but saw no one then stepped behind a large pine and stood still, listening, straining to hear even the slightest movement. Someone was out there watching her. She knew it. She felt it.

She grasped the star in her pocket tighter and quickened her pace back down the path. The sooner she got to Cayman and the warehouse below, the better. About halfway down the mountain, she saw a movement in the shadows. Slowing, she peered through the dense foliage, inching forward, thankful for the soft carpet of pine needles beneath her feet. Cayman stepped out from behind a tree, then paused, as still as the night.

"Jesus, Cay," Xana whispered. "What's up with the theatrics?"

"No theatrics. But a little less noise would be nice."

She narrowed her eyes into fine feline slits. "Why did you drag me all the way out here?"

"It's your birthday. I wanted to give you a present."

"And you couldn't have given it to me, say at the Chart House over a filet?" she asked.

He shoved his hand in his pocket then pulled out a pewter tube with an amethyst crystal set into its top dangling from a long silver chain.

Her annoyance evaporated. "Wow, Cayman." She cupped the necklace in her hand. "It's beautiful."

"I thought you'd like it." He placed it around her neck. "But this isn't all I got you."

"No?" She looked at him warily. Surprise gifts weren't like Cayman.

"You got the pack I asked you to bring?"

"Of course." She patted the strap slung over her shoulder.

"Good. Then let's go."

"Cay." She stopped him with a hand on his arm. "What aren't you telling me?" A niggling in her gut hinted that there was more going on here than he was letting on.

The small muscles in his jaw twitched. "This is a big one."

Xana paused at the slight quiver in his voice. Was it possible that her steadfast older brother, who was always in control, was suddenly afraid? A twinge nipped Xana's insides. She had an intimate relationship with fear, had lived with it for so long, she wasn't sure she could live without it. Cayman, on the other hand, was never afraid and Xana had come to depend on him to keep her fear at bay.

Now she didn't know what to think. "What big one?"

"You'll see."

He was being cryptic again. As they walked farther down the hill, the warehouse came into view. They watched for a moment as the building's front door opened and a young woman stepped out. She locked the door behind her then crossed the empty lot to her red car. "She should be the last one," Cayman said. "They worked late tonight."

Xana felt that odd tingling on the back of her neck again. She swung around, certain there must be someone behind her, but again saw no one.

She was just jumpy. Jumpy and tired.

"Great, now would you mind telling me what's going on?" she asked.

"Vampires. Lots of them."

"Since when do vampires play corporate business? You've got to be wrong about this." God, she hoped he was wrong about this.

"If I'm wrong, then why is your vampire sense doing the tango up and down your spine?"

He was right. She didn't like the uneasiness twisting

through her. Usually they waited until nightfall, hunting vamps in the shadier districts of San Francisco, where the fog crawls across the ocean and winds through the streets. The city was a haven for alternative lifestyles and underground clubs where patrons often offered up the sweet drink willingly. In these haunts, vampires blended in, melded, thrived.

Warehouses in the middle of the mountains were not their normal stomping grounds, but one thing Xana knew about her brother was that Cayman was seldom wrong. His facts were always straight. He took time to make sure they were on the right trail, that their raids were organized and plotted down to the slightest detail.

Xana, on the other hand, was not a thinker, but a doer. A woman of action. And that's what she wanted to do right now—act. Not sit around here watching the shadows deepen into sharp points on the side of an ugly grey box. But still, something didn't feel right about this.

As the red compact disappeared up the road, Cayman turned to her. "Okay, let's go."

"Finally," she said on a deep breath. They hurried down the hillside and into the parking lot then ran toward the building's entrance.

Cayman pulled a key out of his pocket and unlocked the glass front door. "Getting a copy of the key off the woman who just left last night was easy. Getting the codes to the alarm system wasn't. But I got 'em."

An anxious twinge pinched Xana's side. "You've done a lot of planning for this one," she said, wondering why he hadn't clued her into the job earlier.

"Always do." He opened the door and stepped inside then stopped and punched the alarm code into a small box on the wall by the door.

Xana pulled out her gun specifically equipped with wooden-core silver bullets then followed her brother into the heart of the building, down one gloomy corridor after another where the only sound was the low hum of the air conditioner reverberating around them. "Sure is quiet," she whispered.

"Just wait until dark. That's when the party starts." They passed through the main warehouse, weaving through wooden crates stacked ten and twenty feet high. "This place fronts as an import/export business—junk art, vases, statues, but the real work goes on in a lab dug into the side of the mountain."

Xana paused outside a locked door and waited for Cayman to open it. This was way beyond the vamp-staking they usually did. Cayman continued through the doorway, down a long corridor, to a door set into the far wall. Once opened, he stepped out onto a metal landing. Xana followed, then stopped. Her breath catching in her throat choked her. "My God."

The entire floor below them was lined up with row upon row of stainless steel cylinders.

"High-tech coffins," Cayman explained.

Xana turned to him. "Are you kidding me?"

Cayman's gaze hardened. "Does it look like it? According to my sources, someone is building an empire of vampires. We're here to stop them." Cayman descended the stairs, taking them two at a time.

What sources? Xana stared after him. The niggling fingers of concern she'd felt earlier grew into fists of fear. She looked out at the sea of coffins. This was a lot bigger than annihilating a few vamps.

Cayman stopped at the bottom of the stairs and turned back, his eyes darkening as he grasped the rail with whitened knuckles. "Start unloading the explosives. I'll be right back. I just need three minutes, five tops. Then we'll blow this place to kingdom come."

Xana nodded, but realized with certain dread that it hadn't been fear earlier on the hillside that had caused the quiver in Cayman's voice, but rage. Mr. Cool was about to lose it and that scared Xana a lot more than the roomful of vampires below her.

The sooner they got out of this place, the better.

She grabbed Cayman's pack and moved quickly through the room, strategically placing sticks of dynamite in each corner before inserting the blasting caps and running the fuse the length of the room to connect with a detonator. She attached the timer and placed it at the bottom of the stairwell. The explosion had to be powerful enough to incinerate the basement's occupants without bringing down the building or the mountain.

After she positioned her last explosive, she pulled a nearby box next to a coffin and stepped up to look through the small glass window in the top of the steel dome. A man lay tucked inside, his skin an odd shade of purplish gray, the dark circles beneath his closed eyes a deep red. Strangely, he didn't look like a soulless evil vampire, but she knew too well that looks could be deceiving.

She headed back toward the stairwell, winding her way through the coffins until she reached the archway her brother had disappeared through. She looked at her watch. Almost dark. She'd hate to be stuck in this building once those coffins started to open. Even her specialized vamp-blaster wouldn't stop the number of undead housed in this crypt.

"Cayman, come on!" she called down the hallway her brother had disappeared into. She heard a soft footstep behind her and pivoted, her gaze searching the room. Nothing. Her stomach churned. Something moved just outside her field of vision. A blurred shape darted from one coffin to the next, where it slipped out of sight again. Xana stilled, her breath coming in short, quick gasps.

She clutched her gun in both hands and stepped forward, peering behind a row of coffins. A long black leather coat billowed from behind a canister. She'd seen that coat before, knew that mass of jet-black hair. Her blood thinned and rushed to her head.

Marius. King of the vampires. And the one she'd never been able to get near.

The sound of a lock clicking open echoed through the room. Her muscles tensed. Fear, her closest friend and staunchest enemy, grasped hold of her heart and squeezed, wrenching free a flood of adrenaline to buzz through her veins. She ran, rounding the last row of coffins, following that jacket.

No one was there.

Where'd he go?

A breath lifted the hair about her ear.

Xana spun round.

In a quick movement, Marius wrenched her gun out of her hand. His jet-black eyes locked onto hers and, for a second, she couldn't turn away. She was lost and drowning in those inky black pools. Heat flamed, rising through her body to balloon in her chest. Her breath came in short little gasps. She moistened her lips, not missing the quick movement of his eyes as they watched her. She shoved a hand in her pocket and grasped one of the stars, wanting to pull it out, wanting to flick her wrist and embed the razor-sharp points in his chest.

But she didn't.

She couldn't.

Marius wasn't any ordinary bloodsucker. Marius was the king of the bloodsuckers and he hadn't survived as long as he had without learning a few tricks.

Tricks she was pretty sure she didn't want to see.

"Where's Cayman?" His smooth voice moved through her sweet and thick, like hot creamy chocolate, coating her senses, making her want to hear more, making her want to lean in close to see if his breath smelled as sweet.

Jesus, what was wrong with her?

"Where's the cylinder?" he demanded.

"What are you talking about?" Her voice wasn't her own. It was higher, pitchy, weak. She didn't like it.

She didn't like anything about this.

His hardened gaze narrowed as it followed the path of explosives set around the room. "You and your brother won't like the consequences of this game you're playing."

She should have laughed at his threat. Should have come back with something witty, something perfect that would let him know that she wasn't afraid of him. That she could take him down any moment she chose to. But for some reason her tongue was tied.

A cacophony of locks springing open rumbled through the air. Xana gasped then glanced down the hallway, looking for Cayman once more. When she turned back, Marius was gone. That was her cue to leave. She turned and headed for the stairs. She'd wait for Cayman upstairs, away from these coffins. Away from Marius.

"You ready?" Cayman asked, seemingly coming from nowhere.

Xana grabbed him by the arm. "Damn you, Cayman. Where have you been?"

"Getting this." He held up a small plastic case. "Are the charges placed?"

"Yes, but we've got company—Marius. He took my gun, and for some reason he was asking for you and for some kind of cylinder."

Cayman's blue eyes swept the room. Only they weren't quite the blue they'd always been. Somehow they were different, almost mirrorlike and incandescent. "What's up with your eyes?" she demanded.

"What?" Cayman asked, taking a step back.

"I don't know. They look—" she groped for the right word "—pale."

Cayman blinked and he was her brother again, the same guy who had always been there for her—on the day she was born and on the afternoon their parents died. "We'd better move." He glanced furtively around him.

"You got that right."

"Set the charges then meet me back at the top of the road." He placed a plastic case into the pocket of her blouse inside her jacket. "Make sure nothing happens to that case. Trust no one." Cayman turned and started up the stairwell.

"What? Cayman? Damn."

A loud sound popped, then the whoosh of vacuum-released hydraulics. One by one, the coffin doors opened.

"Shit!" Xana ran to the timer hooked to the fuses

that was spread across the room and activated the clock preset to count down from three minutes. "Time to roll."

She saw Cayman flying up the stairs, taking them three at a time. Xana followed, but couldn't catch up as they hurried up one flight after another. She ran through the warehouse past the boxes of junk art and vases. At the other end of the room, Cayman burst through the door into the front offices. Xana glanced at her watch as she followed. "Twenty-five seconds 'til the blast."

She bolted forward, running down one hallway and then another before finally pushing through the offices as shock waves ripped through the building. She tore out the glass front door, covered her head and kept running. The blast shook the ground beneath her. She faltered, trying to find her footing.

A violent roar cracked the sky. Windows shattered. An intense wave of heat slammed into her, lifting her off her feet and throwing her to the ground. Birds took flight with raucous screeches and squawks. Glass and debris pelted her neck and shoulders. After a moment, the ground settled and the clamor dimmed to a chorus of creaks and groans of tortured metal.

Xana lay beneath a bush and took mental inventory of her extremities. She hurt everywhere, her ears rang, her eyes stung. When the smoke thinned, she stood on wobbly legs and looked around her. Her heart dropped, dread filling the empty space. Cayman wasn't in the parking lot or lying on the hillside or anywhere.

"Cayman!" she yelled, and limped stiffly toward the building. She looked through the shattered, gaping opening. He was nowhere to be seen.

Intense panic gripped her. She headed around the back of the building. A side door flew open in front of her. Smoke billowed out the doorway. Marius, his black eyes glowing red, stormed out the door. Stunned, Xana stopped. Before she could catch her breath, he was gone.

She kept walking. Where was Cayman? He'd been ahead of her. He had to have gotten out, unless there was something else he'd wanted to do. She entered through the side door into the building once more and immediately doubled over. The room was a shambles, burning walls and equipment released noxious gasses. High-pitched screams filled the air—vampires succumbing to the flames.

Xana hurried back out the door and up the road toward her truck. Cayman said he'd be there. But he wasn't. There was no sign of him anywhere. Had he left on his own? Without her? That would have been shitty, but she wanted to believe it because the alternative was not something she could grasp. Her brother was nose-deep into something and from the look of things, it wasn't something good.

Trust no one.

She recalled his last words and shivered.

CHAPTER TWO

AFTER a moment of waiting by her truck, Xana turned and hurried back down the hill toward the warehouse. Cayman could not have just disappeared. He had to be here. Somewhere. The building's automatic fire sprinklers had extinguished most of the flames. She poked around inside the building, looking over cubicle walls, under desks and fallen partitions, looking for Cayman. He must be there.

But he wasn't.

Her heart constricted with fear. He had been in front of her. He had to have gotten out. Unless he couldn't. She turned a corner and ran straight into Marius. Without thinking and with an anxiety-laden roar, she launched herself on him, stake in hand. "Where is he?" she demanded.

Marius grabbed her by the neck and pushed her against the wall. She leveraged the stake between them and pushed it against his chest. "Let me go," she threatened.

"You first."

"Where is my brother?"

"Where is the formula?"

This couldn't end well. "I don't know what you're talking about. Now let me—"

The next thing she knew she was flying through the air as if she weighed no more than a child's toy. She hit the wall with a teeth-chattering thud then slid to the floor. She waited for the stars to stop circling then with a derisive shake, pushed to her feet. Damn, she wished she had her gun.

"You should have played possum," Marius scolded, his lips curving into a smile, revealing sharp white teeth elongated into fine chiseled points.

"What fun would that be?" Xana picked up a broken wooden leg from a chair and thudded it against the palm of her hand. God, she looked stupid. Like this little piece of splintered wood would stop someone as old and strong as Marius, but she wasn't about to stand there and let him think of her as a weak little girl he could easily whip. Even if he could.

She drew back and bent low, her weight evenly distributed on the balls of her feet as she contemplated what she should do next and how the hell she was going to get out of there. In an instant, Marius had her once more shoved against the wall, her feet dangling mere inches above the ground. Long fingers gripped her neck, and squeezed. The broken leg dropped to the floor with a loud clatter.

"Are you going to make me ask again?"

"I don't know," Xana spluttered. She knew he had the strength to snap her neck with no more effort than snapping a decayed twig. But he wouldn't as long as he thought she could help him.

She squirmed in his grasp. Marius's grip tightened. "If you don't want me to dismember you, finger by finger, limb by limb, while you lay on the ground screaming for your daddy, then give me the cylinder."

Xana didn't doubt for a second that Marius would live up to his threat. "What's so important about this cylinder?"

Marius leaned in close, his lips mere inches from hers, his black gaze warming her skin, even as she refused to look into it. Lesson 101 in dealing with vampires—never look them in the eyes unless you want your free will pulverized to mush. But she had to breathe, and Marius's breath smelled sweet as it filled her mouth and nose and slowly moved down her throat to expand in her lungs.

Xana gagged, trying to stop the sensation crawling through her. Marius was an old vampire and the most powerful she had ever run across. He had tricks up his sleeve that would make her head spin. Languid warmth coursed through her, relaxing her muscles, easing her mind. For a second, she actually believed everything was going to be okay.

"What are you doing to me?" She tried to pull away, to escape the sickly sweet odor, but only succeeded in butting the back of her head against the wall.

A sharp sting pierced her skin as he sank his fangs into her neck. The sensation burned hot, lighting a fire in her veins as Marius's mouth worked against her throat, sucking, pulling as he drank. A sudden eroticism swept over her, and against her will, against every fiber in her being, she felt desire surge, riding her heated blood as it pulsed through her veins.

She fought it with every ounce of willpower she had, but to no avail. Marius laughed, the sound rumbling deep in his throat and vibrating against her chest.

"I love this. Xana Scorpio, fearless vampire hunter, is now pinned against the wall, helpless against my ministrations. Are you afraid of what I might do to you? Afraid of the sensations flooding though your very human body?"

"Go to hell!"

He laughed again, obviously enjoying himself. "Humans really are victims of the blood coursing through them, flowing and ebbing like the tide. You don't have nearly as much control or power over yourselves as you think you have. But you try, you fight, you play, making the game oh, so sweet."

Xana watched the blood lining the inside of his lips drip down the side of his mouth and knew it was her own. He wiped the crimson liquid off his chin then sucked it off his finger. "I love the taste of you."

Xana's chest tightened with revulsion…and fear.

"I love how you taste so similar to your brother."

Rage laced her mind, spinning it out of control. Had Marius snatched Cayman from the warehouse? Had he killed him while she'd been lying in the bushes outside? How long had she been there? Seconds? Minutes?

Marius bit her again, and this time, as he drank, a peaceful, languid sensation came over her. Even as she pushed against his rock-solid chest, a part of her wanted to throw in the towel, to let her eyes drift closed and sleep—to join her parents in whatever hell existed beyond this place, even if it was nothing but a deep yawning abyss of darkness.

Marius released her and Xana slumped to the floor. Sensations flooded back—fear, anxiety, rage—while dizziness swam through her head.

The sound of approaching sirens painfully pierced her temples.

He shoved his hand inside her breast pocket, his hard grasp scraping against her tightened nipple. "Cayman put a case in this pocket. Where is it?"

Xana turned surprised eyes on her empty pocket. Good question.

"It was the case for the blasting caps I needed to detonate the explosives," she muttered, hoping he'd believe her. Hoping he'd let her go. He didn't. Disoriented and confused she looked up at him, as his tight grasp on her neck cut off her circulation. Her vision wavered as darkness encroached. She couldn't think. Couldn't breathe.

And then there was nothing.

As the sirens grew louder with the approach of the fire trucks, Marius picked up the woman and quickly disappeared into the woods, heading down the mountain to where his car was parked. He didn't know what Cayman and his sister were up to or why they were here, but he'd make them sorry they blew up his warehouse. That formula had been inside and the two annoying humans had obviously beat him to it. But if Cayman ever wanted to see his dear sister again, he would return it. And quick.

Marius had to get that formula for the virus to his people tonight before this situation got any worse. He'd had to kill three of his brethren last night. Who knew how many more were infected. He didn't have the time or the patience to play the human's game.

He resisted the urge to push the accelerator to the floor as he navigated the winding road, passing one emergency vehicle after another. He almost wished he could stick around and see what lies the humans would tell each other about what they were about to discover in the basement of the warehouse. Fire was a great cleanser, but it wouldn't erase everything.

When Marius first learned about the Alliance and their virus, he hadn't believed it could be true. Why should he? The arrogance. The audacity of humans thinking they could conquer the vampire. That they could mimic the genetic structure and create "super" humans. It was ridiculous.

But he'd seen the coffins and the abominations within them. But so far, he'd yet to see a human survive the experiments. Still, he was more concerned about what was happening to the vampires that had been lured into their plan. Somehow the experiments had infected them with a virus that replicated and destroyed, turning friends into vicious, rabid killers with no soul, no conscience, no semblance of who they really were.

He had to stop it.

But to do that he needed the formula from the experiments the Alliance had been conducting. He needed that cylinder. And he would get it, because he knew Cayman well enough to know there was only one thing in this entire world that man valued and Marius had just dumped it in his backseat.

The pretty little Xana would look nice perched on his hook, now all he needed to do was reel Cayman in.

Xana opened her eyes. The first thing she was aware of was the pain shooting through her skull. The second was the chill seeping into her skin. Her eyes widened. Where were her clothes? She tried to move, but couldn't. Both her hands were tied above her, and each foot was strapped to a bed post by…silk scarves?

Son of a bitch!

The bastard had tied her spread-eagle to the bed.

Panic fired through her mind, zipping across her nerve endings. She writhed, pulling at her restraints. Suddenly, fluorescent light lit the room, burning her eyes and sending a fresh arrow of pain shooting through her temples.

"Oh, good, you're finally awake," Marius said as he walked into the room.

With all the strength in her legs, she pulled at her entrapments and cringed as they tightened around her ankles. Tears of anger and frustration filled her eyes. Furiously, she blinked them back. "Where are my clothes?"

"Does it matter? You look much more beautiful as you are."

She stared down at herself. The only clothing she still wore was her white satin thong. The bastard was trying to make her feel vulnerable. She wouldn't give him the satisfaction. She steeled her eyes and glared at him. "What do you want with me?"

"I want the formula and now that I have you, your brother is going to bring it to me." He walked closer, trailing the tip of his finger up her leg. "How have you been, Xana?"

"Just fine, thanks," she said through gritted teeth.

He sat on the edge of the bed and grinned. It was eerie—seductive, charming and deadly. Monsters should not look so damned hot. Leaning in close, he ran his finger along the groove in her stomach.

"Don't touch me." She said the words softly, but stared at him with such fury her eyes felt like hard-burning orbs in her skull.

She was going to kill him.

"You really are a lovely woman."

She ignored him. He was trying to get to her with his mind games. He hovered closer. She looked at his mouth, his deep red lips, made all the more crimson by the pale tint of his skin. Long dark hair framed his face. His dark eyes were…mesmerizing. Seductive. She glanced away.

"Cayman will bring me the formula, and then he will help me and we will all work together."

"You're lying." She bit down hard on her lip to keep from screaming at him and tasted the tinny metallic flavor of her blood.

He stared at her lip and seemed momentarily distracted.

Damn.

He leaned closer. "Am I? Did you know he told me to meet him at that warehouse? It looks as if he's left us both…hanging."

"Why should I believe you?"

"You're right, why should you? Except now it appears

you might have lost him, too. You might be…alone in the world." There was a tiny glint of pleasure on his face as he said the words.

Had he been responsible for what had happened to Cayman? Had Cayman played some stupid game with Marius and lost? For the first time since she opened her eyes, she felt real grab-you-by-the-guts-and-twist fear. Her outrage and anger evaporated.

"What do you know about my brother?"

"What makes you think I know anything?" Marius laughed, then the smile disappeared and his face turned cold, freezing the blood in her veins. "What do you know about the Alliance?" he asked. "About the warehouse we were in?"

"Nothing." This time she whined. She hated it. Hated that she couldn't hold on to her fury. Hated that the fear was seeping in. She felt a slight tickle on the inside of her thigh and tried desperately to clamp her legs together, but all she succeeded in doing was tightening the restraints around her ankles until they cut off her circulation and burned.

"Don't you and your brother talk?"

"Please, let me go," she pleaded, her bravado vanishing and quickly being replaced by Miss Timid-and-Scared.

He bent his face toward the juncture between her thighs.

"What are you doing?" she cried as panic rose in her throat.

"I love this spot, where the flesh is so soft and creamy."

A flash of burning pain exploded in her thigh. "Stop," she screamed. He was biting her! Tearing into her skin. She ripped at her restraints, thrashing on the bed, trying desperately to pull away from him. The silk ripped, nearly freeing her left leg.

The burning in her thigh dulled, spreading languid warmth through her body. Her muscles relaxed. He continued sucking her thigh, until her breathing became shallow and her breasts swelled, reaching, aching...

A hot tingling ignited beneath the satin thong, and she squirmed, growing light-headed. To her horror, a moan escaped her wet lips. Marius lifted his face from her thigh and stared at her, blood dripping down his chin and landing on the white satin where it pooled and spread into the fragile threads.

She knew she shouldn't look into his eyes, but she was past caring. "Please," she whimpered. Do it again, take more, take her.

Fury lit a fire in his eyes. "The Alliance? The experiments?"

The desire-ridden brain-fog swirling in her mind left her incapable of understanding or caring what it was he wanted. In a movement of extreme speed and dexterity, he was lying on top of her, the weight of his body pressing down on hers. She pushed her hips against him, grinding slightly, trying to find some release to the pressure that was just beginning to subside.

She lost herself in the black pools of his eyes, and knew she was his. Right now, she would do whatever he wanted.

He licked the skin behind her ear, tasting, smelling. "Why didn't Cayman tell you? Did he not trust you?" He pulled the sensitive lobe into his mouth, loving it tenderly with his tongue.

The burning within her grew again, building until she felt she'd explode if he didn't kiss her.

She made soft mewling noises as his tongue slipped from behind his teeth and circled her lips. She arched her back, trying to get closer, trying to draw him into her.

"More," she demanded. She pushed her tongue into his mouth, kissing him hard, tasting, devouring, conquering...

He pulled back. "No."

She looked up at him, trying to catch her breath as mortification set it. She wanted him. She'd begged him. And he'd said no.

"Oh, God," she squeaked.

"Don't worry, darling. You couldn't help yourself. You're only...human, after all."

He left her and started toward the door.

"Wait. You can't leave me here like this."

"Like what? Wanting? Lusting? Craving?"

Yes, craving. "Tied up," she said, her voice barely audible.

"Oh, but I can. And I will, until your brother brings me what I want."

"And if he doesn't?"

"Then you need to think about exactly what you're going to do to help me find him."

"Why would I help you?"

"Because it's the only chance you will ever have to see him or anyone again."

"Great," she muttered as he walked out the door. She pulled her leg against the silk bind that had come loose, and pulled her foot free. She glanced quickly at the door, then tried with the other leg. It didn't budge.

"Great," she muttered again and closed her legs. "Happy birthday to me."

CHAPTER THREE

LEAVING the delectable Miss Xana, Marius walked into the kitchen for a bag of blood. She'd responded to him much more strongly than he'd expected, but what truly surprised him was the way he'd responded to her. It had been a long time since he'd felt such an intense pull toward a woman. Any woman, and a human woman at that. But there was something about the bright spot of crimson on her silky white panties and the smell of her desire that stuck with him, and fueled the rock-hard erection that was pushing uncomfortably against his leather pants.

He should go back in there and give her what she wanted. What they both needed. But that wouldn't accomplish anything. He needed her to trust him, to help him figure out what Cayman was doing in that warehouse. His cell phone buzzed. He pulled it out of his pocket and answered it.

"There's a problem at Crank it Up." Jaz, his first sergeant in control of District 3, almost never called. He liked to handle things on his own, and Marius liked to let him. Sometimes. But after what had happened with his three brethren last night, and then not finding the formula at the warehouse tonight, he didn't want to hear any more bad news.

"What kind of problem?"

"A few of our own are out of control."

A few? "Can't you handle it?" Marius barked, clearly annoyed.

"Maybe. There are a lot."

Marius stilled. "How many?"

"Last count…at least six. But more are coming in."

Damn it. What was going on in his city? "All right. I'm coming."

But he wouldn't be going alone. Miss Xana needed to see for herself what they were up against and what the stakes would be if she didn't help him find her brother and that formula.

He gathered up her clothes, walked into the room and threw them on the bed, then quickly untied her silk binds. "Get dressed. We're going into the city."

Instantly, she pulled her clothes in front of her using them as a shield. "I'm not going anywhere with you."

"Do you really think you have a choice? You can either come of your own free will, or I can make you. Now which would you prefer?"

"Why are you doing this?"

"Because I don't have time for games. The Alliance has waged war against us."

"I don't even know what this Alliance is."

"Your brother does. If he kept it from you, that's your problem. You are going to help me find out exactly what he and this Alliance are up to."

"I'm not helping you do anything," she hissed and sputtered, as if she were a wet little kitten. He could almost smile, if he weren't so damned annoyed.

"Fine, then stay here tied up in the dark and maybe I'll come back for you. Or maybe I'll just leave you here to rot." He picked up a silk scarf then grabbed her ankle and yanked it toward him.

"No. Wait. Don't."

He continued tying her other ankle and her wrists.

"You're not serious," she asked, her eyes growing wide.

"I don't have time or patience for your silly antics." He walked out the door, flicking off the light as he did.

"Wait!" she screamed.

He hesitated, opening the door a crack.

"All right, I'll help you. Just don't leave me here."

Within seconds, he had the ties off her ankles and

wrists, and then he tossed her naked body over his shoulder on the way to his car in the garage.

"Put me down," she yelled, as she beat on him, her small pert breasts bouncing against his back, her lovely round backside up on his shoulder next to his chin. For a second he was tempted to take a small nip, but he didn't. Not now. But he would have his pleasure with this woman and her mass of blond hair before the night was over, of that he was certain.

Anger and humiliation burned through Xana as Marius's hand slipped over her bare butt. As soon as she got away from this monster and back to her house, she was going to burn every one of her thongs, and then she'd come back for him. She'd make him pay for this if it was the last thing she did.

If she got out of here.

"Damn you, Cayman," she gritted under her breath. Why the hell would he arrange to meet Marius at the warehouse, then run off and leave her there?

Marius dumped her into the backseat of the Jaguar and tossed her clothes on top of her. "Get dressed."

"Why? I thought you liked me naked?" she snapped.

His eyebrows quirked and she thought she saw the corners of his mouth lift before his face became impassive again and he looked once more like what he was—a stone-cold killer. A monster.

Xana sat in the back of the sleek Jaguar as it roared down the winding mountain road toward Highway 101 and into the city. She pulled her cami over her head, then quickly buttoned her blouse over it and wiggled into her skinny jeans. She cringed as the denim scraped against the bite marks on her upper thigh.

Hate and revulsion flooded through her, filling every molecule of her being. She'd kissed him. His bite put some kind of twisted disgusting vampire spell on her and she'd wanted him to kiss her back. To touch her. Hell, to screw her.

Damn, she wanted a shower. A long, hot shower with a stiff brush. But no. She was stuck in this plush car going with him to God knew where for God knew what. Chances were she'd never see a shower again. Or Cayman. The desperate thought crept unbidden into her mind. She pushed it away. Cayman wouldn't have left her there with Marius. He couldn't have set this all up. Vampires lie. They cheat and they manipulate. And they hypnotize women into kissing them and Lord knew what else. She thought of Marius's hand touching her body and shivered.

"Where are we going?" she blurted, trying to get the thought out of her head.

"Into the city," he answered as they raced through four full lanes of traffic toward the Golden Gate Bridge.

"Why?"

"Because I want you to see firsthand what the Alliance is doing."

"I've already told you I don't know anything about this Alliance."

"Then your brother has done you a great disservice."

Has he? They drove in silence as they entered the city, following the freeway onto Lombard Street then dropping down Van Ness toward the Tenderloin District. Oh, this wasn't good. He pulled to a stop near Seventh Street, outside of several dark and dilapidated warehouses. She looked around, desperately searching for a way to escape, a way to disappear. But here, a woman on her own was easy prey. And not just to vampires.

Especially a woman without her gun.

"What are you hoping to show me?" she asked as he cut the engine.

He didn't answer, but got out of the car. Before she could blink, her door was opening. "Let's go," he said.

"Lead the way."

She walked next to him through the darkness, where the red tips of burning cigarettes were the only signs of life lurking in the shadows. Drug addicts and gang members waiting to accost anyone with a quarter in their pocket filled the dark corners where graffiti covered chipped and peeling paint. The smell of vomit and urine tainted the air, and bundled lumps of humanity forgotten and ignored lay in inebriated clumps against the walls and along the sidewalks of the abused and neglected buildings.

They sidestepped the large grates in the cement where fog billowed up, its tendrils wrapping around and swallowing their legs. She walked quicker, following Marius into an abandoned building that practically hummed with the vibrations of the grating music playing within. As she passed through the darkened door where only flashes of multicolored strobe lights lit the room, Xana knew instinctively that she didn't want to be in there.

The air was thick with the smell of cigarettes and marijuana. She slapped a hand against her nose and mouth to keep from coughing. People stood shoulder-to-shoulder, their faces full of gleaming metal exposed in jagged harsh pieces as the light bounced off their kohl-darkened eyes, white powdered skin and hair cut at choppy angles. Yep, exactly what she would expect to see in a place like this. Even gang members might not mess with some of these freaks.

Marius grabbed her arm and dragged her quickly through the room to a long bar in the back. She had to get away from him. But how?

On a stage a band clad in black leather screamed about the glories of suicide and she had to wonder if it was so great, why didn't they do mankind a favor and get it over with already? Marius exchanged a few whispered words with a vampire behind the bar then pulled her toward a staircase in the far corner and ascended into the darkness. She hesitated, not wanting to go up there, but he yanked on her arm, dragging her after him up the stairs and down a long corridor to another room in the back.

Her stomach rolled in protest as a sickly sweet odor reached her. She tried to pull away, but Marius's grip tightened.

"Let me go," she insisted. But it did no good. He continued forward, practically pulling her after him. When they reached the room in the back, she was horrified by what she saw through the gloom of several thick candles in iron stands and sconces around the room. People were laying on chaise lounges, on couches and on the floor in various states of undress. Making out, making love, slobbering all over each other—a sick, virtual orgy of twisting bodies.

But not everyone was moving. Or moaning.

Apprehension twisted in her gut.

"I want out of here," she said and pulled away, trying to wrench free from his grasp. It was no use. Trying to move him was like trying to move a tree. And not just any tree, a giant sequoia.

Marius ignored her protestations and approached the couple closest to them. The man pulled up from the woman's neck and looked up at him, blood covering the bottom half of his face. The woman was dead, her neck half-gone. Xana froze. The vampire wasn't just drinking her blood, he was eating her flesh.

Revulsion ripped through Xana, turning her stomach. She took an immediate step back. The vampire followed her movement, his eyes glowing an odd shade of reddish-amber. Marius thrust something into the man's heart. Surprise filled the vampire's face seconds before he exploded into an obscure puff of ash.

Xana sagged with relief, but it was short-lived. Her eyes adjusted to the gloom and as she looked around her, she realized the room was full of vampires and, by the sickly sweet odor, blood. They didn't seem to just be taking drinks. They were actually feasting. She faltered, falling back against the wall. She couldn't stay here. Terrified, she looked at Marius and started backing toward the door.

In two strides he was on her.

Marius took Xana's stakes out of his inside pocket and thrust them into her hand. Her eyes widened with surprise. "Don't let them near you," he said then moved into the heart of the room.

He saw Lewis, his old friend from back when he'd first come to San Francisco. Lewis was old-world French and an aristocrat. But more than that, he was a gentleman. A man of sophistication. The animal Marius saw before him tearing into a human like a wild dog was not his friend. His friend had been stolen by the virus.

Fury tightened Marius's grip on the stake as he plunged it into Lewis—doing what he had to do, doing what Lewis would want him to do and what he'd want Lewis to do to him if their roles were reversed. He put Lewis down like the rabid animal he was.

This virus the Alliance had infected the vampires with was spreading. He had to put an end to it and eradicate those responsible now, or soon there might not be any sane vampires left. Which wouldn't be good for any of them. As quickly as he could, he moved through the room, staking one rabid vamp after another.

Until they became aware of what he was doing.

The vampires stood, rising off the corpses and moving toward him. The darkened room glowed with candlelight bouncing off the reddish-amber sheen of their eyes.

Behind him, Xana gasped. As if frozen, she'd been standing against the wall watching with shocked eyes, but not moving. She moved now, as if someone flipped a switch inside her, and started doing what she did best— killing vampires. Though he doubted she'd ever been faced with so many at one time.

He fought with the speed and strength far superior to many of the vamps in the room, who were at least a century younger than him, and by the time he and Xana were done, there was nothing left but the mangled bodies of the victims.

Sickened by the scene before him and by what he'd had to do to his followers, his vampires from his city, he walked slowly around the room, making sure they were all gone. Xana stood by the far wall, breathing heavily, her hand shaking.

"What are we going to do now?" she asked.

"The human bodies will have to be destroyed. No one can ever know who they were or what had happened to them here."

"It's just so…"

He placed a hand on her arm. "We have to make sure this never happens again. We have to stop them."

Looking somewhat shell-shocked, she looked up at him with wet luminous eyes, her mouth opening as if to form a question, but in the end, she just nodded.

Without saying a word, Xana followed Marius out of the chamber and down the stairs to the room below, where people danced and drank and laughed and had no idea of the horror going on above them, or how close they'd come to becoming meat for the monsters around them.

But they were all gone now. Dead because of Marius. She watched him as he whispered in the ear of a bartender, telling him how to dispose of the bodies, she supposed. The vampire nodded, his face looking grim. Then they were out of the warehouse. She took a deep breath of the night air, which now seemed suddenly refreshing. She stopped herself from running down the street toward the docks, where the icy wind and briny, oily smell of the bay could wash her feverish cheeks and clean the scent of death from her nose.

But she knew she would never forget the stench of it.

"What happened back there?" she asked, her voice sounding weak and broken.

"The vampires were infected. They had to be put down."

"Infected?" Uneasiness squirmed through her.

"By a virus created by the Alliance."

She didn't understand. How could a virus cause this kind of horror? What would Cayman know about any of this? Why would he ask Marius to meet him at the warehouse only to blow it up and disappear? And leave her behind?

Suddenly, Marius stopped and turned to her, his dark angry gaze locking onto hers. "Why don't you know anything about this? I thought you and your brother were a team. A vampire-killing, monster-stomping team." His words were loud and mocking. They made her cringe. But he was right. She and Cayman were a team. So, why the hell was he working on this without her?

"I think it's time you tell me everything," she said.

Obviously, he was upset. He'd been telling her the truth. She knew that now. And more than that, she knew she had to help him. What she'd just seen could never happen again. If there was a virus, then it had to be found and it had to be stopped. Obviously, Cayman believed that, too. So where the hell was he?

"In the last couple days, there have been reports of vampires out of control. Killing without regard to detection and eating pieces of their victims." His mouth hardened as he said the words. "This is not normal vampire behavior."

Her uneasiness grew to full-blown anxiety. "There is normal vampire behavior?" she asked before she could stop herself. Then could have slapped a hand over her snarky mouth.

Marius turned away, moving quickly up the street toward his car. She ran forward and grabbed his arm. "Wait. I'm sorry. Please, continue."

His anger, thick and deadly, rolled off him. She dropped her hand and took a quick step back.

"I'd discovered the Alliance has been working on a virus made of vampire DNA that they've been giving to humans."

"Why?"

"Because they want our strength, our speed, our agility."

"Without the blood."

"Without the blood," he repeated. "I don't want to have to kill any more of my people."

For a moment his eyes softened, and she thought she saw pain there. But that couldn't be right. Marius didn't feel. Didn't care. Did he?

She thought of the bodies she'd seen in the warehouse earlier that evening. She thought they were vampires, but if what he was saying were true... "The coffins? Earlier this evening. In the warehouse?"

"They weren't all vampires. Some were human."

"I blew up humans?"

"Does it make any difference? They would have died anyway. No one has survived the process."

"The vampires have."

"If you call what they're turned into surviving. There's nothing left of who they were."

Xana shuddered. It was too horrible to contemplate. "What are you going to do?" she whispered.

"Cayman must have taken the serum the Alliance is using. Without that formula, I'm not sure what I can do."

"Did he tell you who the Alliance is?"

"No."

"I don't understand. Why didn't he tell me any of this?"

"Maybe he didn't want you involved." He started walking forward again, walking away from her.

"If he didn't want me involved then why did he call me and tell me to meet him at that warehouse?"

He spun on her, red fury burning in his eyes. "No, the question you should be asking, is where the hell is he, and why did he leave you with me?"

She shuddered again but this time from fear. She clenched the stake still glued to the palm of her hand, but knew after what she'd just seen it would be of little use to her. "What are you going to do?" she asked again. "With me?"

"I haven't decided," he said, and she realized he was being completely honest. In fact, he'd been honest with her from the start.

"I'll help you," she blurted, without thinking.

He didn't say anything, just stared at her, his face expressionless.

"Not only do I need to find Cayman, but I need to know what he was in to," she said.

"Okay, where do you want to start?" he said, finally speaking.

"Let's go back to Cayman's house and see what we can find."

"All right." He stepped back and gestured for her to precede him.

She shivered as she watched him. The monster was suddenly a gentleman.

CHAPTER FOUR

XANA couldn't help the hope expanding within her as they turned down Cayman's street. She hoped he would be home, that his lights would be on and that he'd have a damned good explanation for where he'd been and what all this Alliance business was about. Marius parked the Jaguar along the curb beneath a large oak across from the well-kept bungalow, which had been built in the forties. But Cayman's house sat in darkness.

"Maybe he's asleep. Or hurt," she said, though she didn't expect Marius to answer. He hadn't said a word on the drive back across the bay. They slipped from the car and hurried toward the house. Sodium vapor lamps spaced few and far between cast long shadows on the large bushes of blooming hydrangeas flanking the front walk on either side of Cayman's small porch. They bypassed the walk, soundlessly skirting around the side of the house toward the back.

The gate in the tall fence opened easily. They followed a serpentine brick walkway, entered a small backyard and glanced in the windows as they passed but saw nothing. Xana approached the back door, took out her keys and opened it.

They entered a small dark kitchen. Anxiety had her nerves jumping as they quickly checked the house. There was no sign of Cayman anywhere, nor any sign that he'd been there recently. Xana sighed and flipped on a few of the lights. "He's not hiding or hurt. He's just not here."

Without uttering a sound, Marius opened cupboards and drawers and flipped through papers and envelopes on the counter.

"What are you looking for?" she asked, not bothering to hide her annoyance.

"Anything that can tell me about the Alliance."

Could this Alliance be so bad that Cayman wanted to protect her from it? Was that why he'd kept her in the dark? He should have known better. She could take care of herself, she would have thought the last two years they'd spent hunting vampires together would have proved that. And besides, working in the dark put her at risk. Obviously.

She searched the living room but found nothing. She started to move into the bedroom when she heard a movement by the back door. She stilled, then turned to Marius, lifting her finger to her lips, giving him the quiet signal. She gestured toward the bedroom.

Marius raised his eyebrows, an amused grin tilting his lips. She stopped for a second. She'd never seen him smile, really smile. It changed his whole face, turning him from someone who gave her the willies to someone she might be interested in knowing. The effect was disconcerting to say the least.

Go, she mouthed silently and shooed him away. Surprisingly, he did as she asked and stepped into the darkness behind the opened bedroom door.

She crept toward the kitchen and was surprised to see Uncle Ben opening the back door. She hadn't seen her uncle since Christmas. What could he be doing here now? And creeping in the back door?

"Hi, Uncle Ben. What's up?" she said loudly, though she didn't need to. Vampires had exceptional hearing. Smiling widly, she stepped into the kitchen.

Uncle Ben looked stunned to see her. "I…uh… I'm looking for Cayman."

And you couldn't knock on the front door? "I'm afraid he's not here. Is there anything I can help you with?"

"No." He hesitated. "He was supposed to meet me earlier and didn't show up, so I thought I'd come back. Do you know when he'll be home?"

"No. What was he supposed to meet you about?" she asked.

"It's…" He paused. "It's nothing. I'll see you later, Xana." He kissed her on the cheek then walked back out the kitchen door, closing it behind him.

She stared after him, feeling decidedly shut out. That was definitely odd. What was going on with her family?

"Is something wrong?" Marius asked, suddenly standing behind her.

She turned around and found she was standing too close to him. If she leaned forward, even an inch, her nose would be brushing against the silky fabric of his shirt.

"That was just very strange," she said, slightly distracted by the width of his broad shoulders and the definition of his pecs. "I've never seen Uncle Ben act like that before."

"Like what?"

She took a step back to regain her equilibrium. "I don't know. All distant and unfriendly-like. And since when has he ever had anything to do with Cayman?"

"Are they not close?"

The light bounced off his long deep ebony hair, reminding her of the sheen of a raven's wing. Before this moment, she hadn't noticed how beautiful it was.

"Um. No. Yes. I mean, we lived with him after my folks died, but it's not like we're a warm and fuzzy family. He was always very busy, and now we only see each other on major holidays, like birthdays and Christmas."

"Apparently Cayman wanted to talk to him about something."

"Yep. Apparently." Disconcerted, she turned away. She didn't like noticing his shiny hair or his strong shoulders or how tall and incredibly hot he was. He was a vampire who would bite her and take what he wanted from her in an instant. She couldn't forget that. And if she started to, all she had to do was think of the tender spots at her throat and the top of her thigh.

Which she did and, as she did, heat filled her cheeks as the memory came rushing back. His face nestled in her crotch, the erotic fire his mouth and teeth had drawn out of her. Warmth suffused her chest. Her hand fluttered against it and she let out a deep breath as she hurried toward her brother's bedroom. She had to put some distance between them.

"What does Uncle Ben do?" Marius asked, following her.

Now he wants to talk? She reached the doorway and saw the king-size bed that dominated most of the room, and spun on heel turning back. "He's a doctor at the VA hospital."

Marius walked past her into the bedroom and started rifling through the dresser drawers. She sighed, followed him into the room and checked the nightstand. She needed to focus. They were looking for anything that would tell her about this Alliance group and shine a light into the secrets her brother was keeping.

Marius picked up a picture off the dresser of Uncle Ben and the two of them at Cayman's graduation. "He was hiding something," he said.

"Uncle Ben? Nah. He's a doctor, that's all he's ever wanted to be, all he's ever been, and all he's ever thought about. He doesn't even know your—" she flapped her arm and gestured toward him "—kind even exists."

"You mean bloodsuckers?" he asked, another amused grin curving his lips. The warm cadence of his voice reached inside her, tickling the back of her throat. Apparently he had a sense of humor, too. Along with being undeniably handsome, in a dark, dangerous and totally inappropriate way.

It was just wrong.

"Look, I might not be very close to Uncle Ben but he and Cayman are all the family I have. He's a good man. And more than that, he's my blood. I won't let you hurt him or Cayman."

"Who says I want to hurt them. But I like your spunk, kitten."

"Great," she muttered. Now she was a cute furry thing. Could she be any more insulted?

"And you're right. He is blood. And it's always about the blood, never forget that."

What was that supposed to mean? Her eyes met his and before she knew it, she was stepping into the black heat of his gaze and sinking.

"Blood holds everyone's secrets, their boldest triumphs, their greatest sins." His voice moved through her, caressing her senses with a lover's touch.

"Stop it," she insisted.

"Stop what?"

"Trying to put some kind of hanky-panky spell on me. I'm not going to betray my Uncle Ben. He's a good man. A man who has put his whole world into his work at the hospital."

Once more, a smile lifted his incredibly enticing lips.

"What?" she asked, feeling slightly annoyed. Now he was all Mr. Charming. Well, it wasn't going to work on her. She knew what he was. And she wasn't attracted to him. Not one little bit.

"I don't put hanky-panky spells on people." He stepped closer.

Her breath caught in her throat. "You don't?" Then what was he doing to her?

He leaned forward, hovering so close their lips were almost touching. Her gaze locked onto his as he traced his tongue around the curve of her lips, tasting, tempting her. This couldn't be happening.

She took a quick step back, but her calves hit the side of the bed and she almost fell backwards onto the mattress. That would be bad. Really bad. She grabbed hold of his arm to steady herself. Then his arms were around her, pulling her against his chest. His mouth fell over hers and instinctively her lips parted. He entered, thrusting deep.

She gripped him tighter. A soft moan rose from her chest as she melted into his arms. His kiss was strong and passionate, making her knees weak. She should pull away, but as his lips moved against hers, sparking the smoldering fire deep within her core, she could no more stop him than she could stop the blood rushing through her veins. She succumbed to his touch and melted as his lips blazed a burning trail down her neck.

"We shouldn't be doing this," she said, but then her breath swelled and a slow tingle moved through her breasts until they ached for his touch.

His fingers moved gently down her body, feeling, caressing. All she could do was feel. And want. And need. She moved against him, a dangerous dance, as desire pulsed through her. This was crazy, beyond crazy, and yet, when his fingers stroked her already hardened nipple, all her reservations were forgotten.

She unbuttoned his shirt, pulled it off his shoulders and clamped her mouth over his rosy bud. After a moment of satisfying her need to taste him, she pulled off her blouse and cami, desperate to feel his cool skin next to hers. She'd always heard that vampires were cold, but Marius wasn't. He wasn't hot, nor was he cold. More like cool and satiny smooth. She drew her fingers down his chest, feeling each ridge, each strong muscle beneath the skin. Her hand hovered at the waist of his leather pants then brushed across his thick bulge. Smiling, she pressed her hand against it, knowing it was growing and pulsing just for her.

Marius groaned, lifted her and together they fell onto the bed, his mouth plundering hers once more. A moan erupted from her lips, as his hands cupped her breasts, his fingertips teasing the sensitive skin, his nails gently scraping across her nipples until she thought she'd scream with the delicious torment.

"Oh, yes," she whispered, as heat, anxious and devouring, circled through her, flooding her mind, constricting her lungs until she gasped for air, and her belly was taut with need. She thrust her hips against him. A deep guttural groan rising from the back of her throat.

His erection, hot and thick, met her hips. She unfastened his pants, then reached inside and grasped hold of it, longing to take him full in her mouth, to taste him, to rub the velvety smoothness of his skin across her tongue.

Suddenly, she pulled back, gasping a deep reality-filled breath. What was she thinking? Better yet, what was she doing?

"Is it not good?" he asked, lust hooding his dark eyes.

She almost laughed. Almost. Until he took her hand and kissed her wrist, his tongue sweeping across her pulse point. "Oh, it is very good." She sighed. "Too good."

"And what is wrong with that?"

"Um. Well…"

His lips followed a torturous path up her arm to the base of her neck, drawing a deep breath from her as she fought to maintain control when all she really wanted to do was wrap herself around him and lose herself in his touch.

"You are a vampire." She said the words out loud, hoping they'd sink into her desire-laden brain.

"Yes." He pulled the sensitive skin of her throat into his mouth and sucked until she thought she'd climb right up the wall.

"You could bite me." Especially the way he was positioned right now. She really should make him stop, but honestly, what he was doing felt so damned good she just couldn't bring herself to care.

"Yes. I could. Do you want me, too?"

"No." She planted her hands on his chest and started to push.

"No? A lot of women like it. They find it very…satisfying." He leaned over her, looking down into her eyes. "It could be very good. For both of us."

He bent down and licked her breast, circling her nipple. Oh, shit. Her back arched as pleasure shot through her. She was hopeless. Lost. A fool.

And at this moment, she didn't care.

Within seconds he had her pants off and he was stroking her tender swollen flesh that was so desperately aching for his touch. He left a trail of hot kisses down her torso, toward her heat. She closed her eyes, all protestations over as the warmth of his mouth, the soft wetness of his tongue circled around her most sensitive spot, taking her in his mouth and lightly flicking his tongue back and forth.

White-hot heat shot through her and she lost it, slipping into an orgasm so strong, she screamed aloud, her body lifting off the bed, her heart pounding as adrenaline surged through her. Before she could recover, she felt the long, thick length of him sliding into her.

She wrapped her legs around him and lifted herself off the bed, taking all of him deep into her. "Sweet mercy," she groaned, and closed her eyes as he started to move, his hips bucking and rocking until she was teetering on the edge once more, until with one final thrust, she exploded again and again, until she was nothing but putty in the palm of his hand.

When her eyes finally opened, she didn't know how much time had elapsed but her heart rate had slowed and her breathing had returned to normal. She turned to look at Marius, not sure what she'd find—the man with eyes filled with ice or liquid pools of languid heat. His dark gaze bore into hers and she closed her eyes as he leaned close and brushed his lips against the corner of her mouth.

"I did not bite."

She smiled. "It's a good thing. I don't think my heart could have taken any more."

He kissed her again softly, sweetly. "It can. You'll see."

Warmth shot through her once more. "Is that a promise or a threat?"

"Stick around and find out."

She sighed as his tongue caressed her lips. "I do so like a challenge."

"But not now." He pulled back and climbed off the bed, leaving her reaching for him.

"Why not?" she asked.

"Because right now we're going to visit the VA hospital."

"The VA hospital?" she repeated, then sat up and swung her legs off the bed. "Why?"

"Because those men in the coffins you blew up this evening looked a lot like soldiers."

CHAPTER FIVE

"You think my uncle…?"

"Whoever is doing this is trying to create super humans." Marius pulled on his shirt and reached for his pants.

"As in super soldiers? But my uncle is a good man." Xana thought of the way Uncle Ben had taken in her and Cayman after their parents' accident. It couldn't have been easy for a single workaholic doctor but he'd done it without blinking an eye. She had a hard time believing it could be possible that he was infecting his own patients. She really wanted to believe in him. He was her family.

"If it's crossed my mind then maybe it crossed Cayman's," Marius said. "Maybe he's there."

"But it's a VA hospital. All you're going to find is sick people."

"Exactly. Sick and desperate people."

Desperate enough to be infected with vampire DNA? She shuddered at the thought, then stood and hiked her blue jeans up over what was left of her thong. "All right, let's do it."

A half hour later they were pulling into the dark almost empty parking lot of the Northern California VA Hospital.

"I think visiting hours are over," Xana said, as they parked the car.

"I'll take care of that," Marius said as he got out of the vehicle.

He must be planning on doing one of his persuading spells on the guard, she thought. Sometimes it was good to have a vampire around. Xana choked. She did not just think that! And yet, somehow, she knew that after this night, nothing would ever be the same. For any of them.

"Are you all right?" Marius asked, as he opened her door.

"Yes, thank you." She took his hand and got out of the car. Look at her being all polite. She sighed. She supposed knock-your-socks-off sex could do that to a girl.

They walked through the front doors and straight toward the guard's desk. Marius was amazing. He just looked at the man and told him what they wanted and the next thing she knew the guard was telling them exactly where to go. Freaky.

And totally disconcerting. If he wanted to, he could make her do anything he wanted. Anything.

Moving at a brisk pace, they made their way down the stairs and into the bowels of the building. The lower they went, the quieter and spookier it was. "I didn't know they had an R and D department here," she whispered, though she didn't know why. There wasn't a soul in sight.

"What better place to perform their experiments?" His mouth twisted in disgust.

Hers did, too, as they passed room after room filled with animals in cages. Xana's heart broke. "I hate this. And I hate that my uncle could be involved."

"Sometimes family is the last to believe and the last to know."

"I must admit, part of me hopes we will find nothing else down here but dusty old filing cabinets and vintage medical equipment."

"And the other part?"

"Hopes we'll find Cayman."

"This way," Marius said, gesturing down another dark hall.

"How do you know where you're going?"

"Call it a hunch."

And then she heard it, the soft moans Marius had probably been hearing all along. Cayman. She rushed forward to the end of the hall to the last windowless room on the left. Cayman lay in a bed, hooked up to various machines and an IV. Forgotten and alone.

"Oh, my God!" She hurried to her brother's side. "What happened to you?"

Cayman turned to her, his skin a purplish gray, his eyes a very pale blue.

She froze as her heart dropped with a heavy thud into her stomach.

Behind her, Marius placed a gentle hand on her back. "He's been infected."

She shook her head in denial. "No."

"It was an accident," Cayman said, his voice gravelly. "Was poking around and touching things I shouldn't have been touching." His eyes drifted closed as if the effort of speaking took more strength than he had.

This couldn't be happening. They had to do something. Marius dragged a chair to the side of Cayman's bed for her. Grateful, she sat down, grasping Cayman's hand with her own. His skin felt dry and cold to her touch. She kept staring at his hand, rubbing her thumb over it, back and forth as a strange numbness came over her. She was shutting down. She could feel her mind closing off like a dark cloud falling over the city, blocking out the sun's light with its thick heavy despair.

He was going to die, a voice inside her whispered, and tears filled her eyes. She rested her head on his hand, feeling his papery skin against her cheek. She took a deep breath, trying to reign in her emotions. She had to be strong for him. She had to make him strong, to help him fight. He could make it through this. He had to.

"What is he doing here?" Cayman asked, looking up over her shoulder.

"Marius helped me find you."

"Can't trust—" A fit of coughs wracked his body, making him visibly weaker.

Xana's stomach twisted into knots. "Cayman, save your strength. We're going to help you."

"Where is the antidote?" he whispered.

She looked at him with confusion then turned to Marius, the question in her eyes. Marius just shook his head. "What antidote?" she asked.

"The case I gave you. It has the antidote in it."

Tears filled her eyes as the horror of his words sunk in. "I don't know. I lost it."

He cringed then started coughing again.

"When did you last have it," Marius asked, his hand a comfort on her shoulder.

"I don't—"

"Don't tell him," Cayman said, his voice barely a rasp. "Don't trust him. He's involved."

She looked up at Marius, Cayman's words making her hesitate. Did she trust him or had he put some kind of mind-spell on her, too? She thought about all they'd been through that night, at the bar, at Cayman's house. He cared about his people, that had been clear. He cared about saving them as much as she cared about finding Cayman. If they worked together, maybe they could save them all.

"I trust him," she said to Cayman.

"Then you're a fool," he replied, his words cutting her to the quick.

"Where is the formula?" Marius asked him. "What did you do with it? We need it to create a vaccine so we can stop the spread of the virus. If we had it, we could make an antidote. We could help you."

Cayman's eyes flashed bright blue. "I had an antidote. It was in the case I gave Xana. I don't have time to wait for you to make another one."

"Why didn't you get it back from me at the warehouse? Why did you disappear?" Xana asked, grasping for understanding.

"I had to go. I was sick and getting sicker. I couldn't let Marius see me. Couldn't take that chance. I waited at the top of the road but then…the explosion. Too…big." He struggled to breathe. "Uncle Ben came out of nowhere…."

"You two are the ones who set the explosives," Marius said.

"Had to. Couldn't let those things loose. Most…were…

vampires. You don't know—" he gasped for breath, his strength waning "—what they're capable of."

"Don't I?" Marius turned to Xana. "When did you last see the case?"

"Xana. Don't. Give him…cylinder. It's all he…wants." A slew of coughs wracked Cayman's chest. Speckles of blood splattered his hospital gown.

"Stop. Cayman. Please. I don't have this cylinder," she protested, her heart breaking into a million jagged painful pieces. "I need to trust Marius. I can't do nothing and just let you die."

"It doesn't matter." He coughed again. "There is no time. Not for me."

"Where is the formula," Marius insisted. "We have to stop the virus from spreading."

"Trust him, Cayman," Xana pleaded.

Cayman lifted himself up and pointed a shaky hand at Xana's neck. Her hand flew to the necklace he gave her. "The formula is inside."

Nausea rolled through her as she took off the necklace and handed it to Marius. She'd had it all this time!

"There, you got what you were after. Now go," Cayman said then fell back against the pillow, his eyes closing once more.

Marius's hand brushed Xana's shoulder. She looked up at him as he gestured for her to follow him into the hall. "You can trust me," he said. "You know that, right?"

She did know it. She nodded.

"Then I want you to remember where you were when Cayman gave you the case. Think about what happened after." She listened to his voice and leaned closer to him, staring into his dark gaze until she felt as if she were drowning. Her tongue slipped out to moisten her lips as she anticipated his kiss, his touch, his taste, knowing he could search her mind for any memories she might have hidden there.

"Please tell me I'm doing the right thing?" she whispered.

"I don't need to. You already know."

He kissed her gently and she felt herself melting as his kiss deepened, as his lips moved behind her ear and down her neck. She didn't feel it coming and barely flinched as he bit her, his fangs sinking into her neck with a sting that quickly melted to pleasure.

Her eyes fluttered closed as heat began to rise within her. Just as quickly, he broke away, releasing her. She grabbed onto his shoulders for support as she wavered in his arms. "Did you see anything?"

"You were running through the building, the case in your hands. The impact from the explosion sent you flying into the bushes. Then you saw me. You got up and ran into the building, looking for your brother, the case forgotten."

"You think it fell into the bushes where I landed?"

"Yes, I'll find it."

"Why didn't you see all that the first time you bit me?"

"I only saw him put the case in your pocket before I broke away."

"Will you go to the warehouse?" She glanced at her watch. "It's only two hours 'til sunrise."

"Xana," Cayman called, his voice barely reaching them. She rushed back into the room.

His eyes widened as his gaze moved to her neck. She touched the wound. Her skin felt wet and sticky.

"It's okay," she assured him. "Marius is going to help us."

"You can't trust him," Cayman muttered. "It was his warehouse we blew up. He's been in on it, working with Uncle Ben from the start."

Shocked, she turned to Marius. "Is that true? Was the warehouse yours?"

"Yes. Just like the warehouse in the Tenderloin is mine, but I don't manage it. And I didn't manage the one you destroyed. One of my sergeants did. That's how I knew there was a problem. He was one of the first infected. He was the one working with the Alliance. It was his blood the Alliance used to create the virus."

Xana turned back to her brother and grabbed hold of his hand. "I never would have found you without him, Cayman. Besides, you are the one who called him and told him to meet you at the warehouse. Why would you have done that if you didn't think he could help us?"

"I didn't call him," Cayman said. "I never would have never done that."

Xana's blood froze. That couldn't be true. Marius told her Cayman had… She turned back to Marius, expecting an answer. An explanation. But he was gone.

And so was the cylinder.

CHAPTER SIX

MARIUS maneuvered the Jaguar down the lonely pre-dawn streets racing toward his mountain warehouse, wondering if he was going to have enough time to retrieve the antidote, deliver it back to the hospital and get back before sunrise. He'd be cutting it close. Too close.

He had to wonder why he was doing it. Cayman and his sister had been a thorn in his side for years. Why not let the boy die? Without him, his sister would move on, get married and settle down with two kids and a white picket fence. No more chasing vampires in the middle of the night. No more chasing him.

But he realized he'd miss her. He'd grown fond of the little hellcat, always hissing and snarling, but when she cuddled up next to him all warm and soft, it gave him a feeling he'd like to explore further. And he couldn't if he let her brother die. He called Jaz and ordered him to rouse their scientist friend and meet him at the warehouse. He only hoped they would get there in time.

He drove down the hill and parked as close to the bushes as he could, shining a light where he believed Xana had fallen. As quickly as he could, he searched the area, checking under bushes as the sky lightened on the horizon. Damn. He was running out of time.

Within minutes he found the case. Inside was a syringe with its barrel full of a gold liquid. He closed the case, jumped back in his car and sped back toward the hospital, calling Jaz once more. "Change of plans, meet me at the VA hospital in the city."

"Have you seen the sky, Marius?" Jaz said.

"If I can make it, you can. Call me when you get there."

Twenty minutes later, Marius pulled into the hospital parking lot. He'd hoped Jaz would have beat him there, but his car was nowhere in sight. He rushed into the building, past the guard, and hurried down into the basement.

"Where's Xana?" Marius asked as he burst into the room. Without waiting for an answer, he took the tip off the syringe and pumped the medicine directly into the catheter already inserted into Cayman's vein.

"My uncle took her."

Marius looked up from the syringe as the last of the

medicine entered into Cayman's bloodstream. "What? Why?"

"He wants the formula back. I told him we don't have it. That we gave it to you, so he took her. Said she was leverage. Though why he thought you'd care enough to exchange the formula for Xana, I don't know."

"You don't think I would?"

"Why would you?"

Why indeed. "How long will it take before you are able to get up out of this bed?"

"I'm not sure. Why?"

"Because the sun's coming up. I'm running out of time. I have maybe ten minutes to find your sister before I need to head back to my resting place. And you, my friend, are going to help me."

"Great. That's your idea of a rescue?"

"Got any better ideas?"

"Give him what he wants."

"And have him turn every vampire in this city into a crazed zombie? Think again."

Cayman blew out a sigh and flexed his hands. "I think it's working."

"Good. Now where do you think he would have taken her?"

"Not far. Uncle Ben knew I was dying, but he didn't know that I've changed in certain ways. Like my sight and my hearing."

"Like a vampire's, eh?"

"It's amazing." Cayman sat up and swung his legs off the bed. "Let's go get my sister."

"Uncle Ben, what in the world are you hoping to accomplish?" Xana asked, straining against the rope he used to tie her hands behind her back. She stared at her uncle, unable to believe the man in front of her was the same one who had bought her her first car and who had been there for her when she needed him.

"I've spent my whole life mending these soldiers, doing everything I could to repair their lives. They come back from duty with a lot more than broken bones, torn ligaments and missing limbs. These men lose so much out there on the battlefields. And for what? Do you think anyone here even understands or appreciates their sacrifice? They deserve more and I can give that to them."

"How? By turning them into monsters?"

"By giving them an advantage, by giving them more than armored cars and vests. With vampire DNA, they can see better, hear better, smell more. They will be faster, stronger, and—"

"Able to leap tall buildings with a single bound. Do you not know how ridiculous you sound? People are dying. And it's all because of you and your insanity."

"People have been dying for years but no one sees and no one cares."

"I understand. And it's terrible. But these men chose

their paths. The ones you've killed had no choice. The vampires you've infected with your virus are murdering people, and that's on your doorstep. You have to stop this. You have to find a different way."

"You should listen to her," Cayman said, stepping into the room and leaning against the doorframe. He looked like Cayman, sounded like Cayman, but his eyes were a startling preternatural blue.

Uncle Ben's gray eyes widened. "How?"

"How did I survive when you, my dear uncle, left me for dead? A vampire saved me."

Uncle Ben was suddenly standing behind her, a scalpel held against her throat. "Give me that formula."

In a flash Uncle Ben was on the ground and Marius was standing behind her, undoing her ropes.

"If anyone is going to tie you up, it's going to be me."

"Promise?" she asked with a wicked smile.

"Can you two do that later? Frankly, it's revolting," Cayman said, and pulled his uncle up from the ground.

"What are you going to do with him?" Xana asked Cayman.

"I'm going to make sure his days of experimentation are over. I'll stay here with him and help him destroy every bit of his data, everything he has on this project, and then he's going to resign from the hospital."

"And if I don't?" Uncle Ben asked with barely re-strained fury.

"Then you will have to answer to the hospital board and eventually the police for what you've done to me, and the other men in the next hall."

Other men? "Will they survive?" Xana asked.

"Yes. I'll make sure of it," Marius said. "But right now, I need to get back to my home. I'd like you to come with me."

"Cayman?"

He nodded. "I'm fine. Go on. We'll be busy here for a long while."

Before she could agree, Marius picked her up in his arms and the next thing she knew they were standing in the parking lot and her head was spinning. A dark sedan approached and the passenger window rolled down.

"Here's the formula," Marius said. "I want an antidote and a vaccine by nightfall."

"I'll see what I can do," a gray-haired man with Coke-bottle spectacles said and reached his hand out the window for Xana's necklace.

"I'll call you tonight, Jaz," Marius said, then they left the hospital with Marius driving like a speed demon as the sky grew lighter and lighter and the horizon exploded in a beautiful display of pinks and oranges.

Xana cringed. "Damn, we'd better hurry."

Xana woke naked on the bed, her hands and feet tied once again to the bedposts and Marius's head nuzzled between her breasts gently kissing and licking. She didn't know whether to be annoyed or excited. Several candles burned around the room, filling the air with the subtle scent of vanilla.

"You're awake," Marius said, and reached for a feather lying on the bedside table.

"You are incorrigible," she murmured as the sensation of wispy softness moved across her skin and sent tingles cascading through her.

"That's what I've been told." He circled her nipple with light feathery strokes.

"Where are my clothes?" she asked on a quick inhale of breath.

"I tossed them. They were filthy."

"Yeah. Well, they've been through a lot." She moaned as he moved the feather between her legs.

"Of course, you have, too. Perhaps you've been tied up enough for one day?" He started to rise.

"Get back here," she said, pulling on her binds as she tried to reach for him.

He bent down and kissed her deep, his tongue doing an erotic dance with hers. "Are you sure? Maybe you've had enough of me?"

"There are parts of you I haven't even begun to explore," she said, her voice low and breathy.

"I might be a little hard to take. I'm known to be demanding. Some might even say, controlling."

"True. But I'm certain there's a lot more to you and I'm willing to spend some time figuring you out."

"Even a monster like me?"

She smiled. "I think I've learned a little more about monsters than I knew before."

He kissed her deeply, stealing her breath, then moved the feather down her body, doing things with it she didn't even know could be done. She gasped a deep breath as fire shot straight to her core, melting her into a puddle of wanton desire.

"I've learned some things, too," he said.

"Oh, yeah," she said on a breathy moan.

"Yeah. Kittens can be fun. I think I'll keep you."

"Well, watch out, baby. I bite."

* * * * *

HER DARK HEART

Vivi Anna

CHAPTER ONE

TREVOR BLACKSTONE rode shotgun in the ambulance as it raced toward the 911 call. It was three in the morning and the streets of Nouveau Monde were still hopping. That was what happened in a city where at least one third of the residents were vampires.

The call came in from Sinsational, a vampire cabaret club that entertained all the other denizens of the European city—lycans, witches, vampires and humans. For the most part it was just some fun, but sometimes it could get out of hand. Hence, 911 had been called. But instead of a blood bite gone too far, they had a 901-a shooting.

When Kostas, Trevor's partner, pulled the ambulance up to the curb in front of the club, there were a couple of police cars blocking off the street. Two constables stood outside the front doors. Trevor got up, went into the back, and opened up the main doors. He jumped down, medical kit in hand, and waited for Kostas so they could lift out the stretcher and take it in.

"Hey, Blackstone," one of the constables said as Trevor and Kostas passed him to go into the club. Trevor nodded to him and continued on.

The club was large, could easily hold three hundred people and usually did most nights. The owner, Mistress Guinevere, was a popular attraction. An eight-hundred-year-old vampiress who could sing like a nightingale. She had a voice like no other. Her songs could move most people to tears, and sometimes into the throes of passion.

Trevor had experienced both.

He'd come to the club a couple of times during his nights off. He'd heard so many things about it, and the proprietor, that his curiosity had gotten the best of him. Both nights had been impossible to forget.

Inspector Gabriel Bellmonte met them about halfway across the floor.

Trevor greeted his friend. "Hey Gabe. What's the situation?"

Gabriel looked at his notebook. "Multiple gunshot wounds. The victim is vampire, no more than seventy-five years old."

"Silver bullets?"

"Yeah."

Trevor and Kostas followed Gabriel down the back stairs to the basement where other more decadent activities took place. At the bottom of the stairs, they stepped into a large room. Trevor could think of only one thing when he searched the room, French boudoir.

The room was decorated in deep rich colors, reds and gold. Each wall was adorned with a nude painting and candelabra flickering with low light. Lounge sofas were set against two walls. On each were three or more loungers. He counted four women and two men. Each was dressed elegantly, lavishly even, as if they were in a Shakespearean stage production. It was totally for show. Vampires didn't dress like this in their usual day-to-day or night-to-night activities.

On the thick white shag carpet lay the victim—a female vampire dressed in a sheer black gown that left nothing to the imagination. Another vampire, a constable, was down on his knees pressing a blood-soaked cloth to the victim's chest and to her stomach.

Trevor crouched beside her, to take her vitals. He nodded to the constable. "What's her status?"

"Gunshot wounds to her chest and stomach. Happened about ten minutes ago. She's been lucid until now."

Trevor examined her pupils, shining a light in them. They still responded, which was good. He then listened to her heart with his stethoscope. Her heartbeat was still strong, considering. Most people thought vampires were the undead, that they didn't have heartbeats or breathe air, but the truth was they were as alive as the rest of humanity. Vampirism was a genetic quirk that could be passed on by blood transfusion—although it was rare for that to happen.

Nudging the constable aside, Trevor looked at the bullet wounds. If he could extract the silver, she'd live. If he couldn't eventually it would kill her. Like poisoning, the silver would eventually dissolve into her bloodstream and stop her heart.

He took out a pair of forceps. Kostas knelt down on the other side of the body and held up a flashlight, a beam directed onto the bullet hole in her chest. Time was of the essence. He couldn't wait a second longer. She was already going into septic shock.

Without a word, Trevor forced the instrument into the hole and rooted around for the bullet. He found it, pulled it out, then moved down to the wound in her gut. He took that one out in less time.

"Will she live?"

Trevor glanced up at the woman standing over them. It was Mistress Guinevere. She was as exquisite as he remembered. Vampires were always beautiful and alluring, but this vampiress took that to a whole other level.

She had waist-length brilliant red hair, amber eyes and pale skin. Most vampires were pale but Guinevere had skin like fine china. She almost glowed.

Nodding to Kostas to bandage her up, Trevor stood. "Yes, she'll live."

"Good. That's good." She wrung her long elegant hands together.

And that's when Trevor noticed the blood drops on her peacock blue gown.

He reached out for her. "Are you—?"

She shook her head, then with a nod, turned to go into the adjacent room. Grabbing his medical bag, Trevor followed her in.

After he stepped over the threshold, the door closed on its own. Although he knew that wasn't possible; the vampiress had likely compelled it shut. Turning quickly, he pulled on the door. It was locked.

"Am I a prisoner?"

"Of course not, I just need some privacy. I don't want the others to know I am injured. It would worry them."

Trevor approached her. "Where are you hurt?"

She lifted her right arm to reveal a bullet wound along her side.

As he neared her, he stripped off the latex gloves he was wearing, shoved them into a pocket, and snapped on a new pair. He inspected the bloody wound. It wasn't as bad as the other vampiress'; this was a through and through. The bullet was not inside her flesh, eating away at her.

"It's not bad. But I'm going to need you to take off

your dress so I can bandage it properly." The dress looked as though it cost about a month of his salary and he really didn't want to ruin it further. "What happened, by the way? How did you get shot?"

From this close proximity, he could see her glorious amber eyes. They sparkled like gems, mesmerizing him. The scent of cinnamon wafted to his nose and he had to fight the urge to inhale deeply.

"Someone with a vendetta I think. I don't believe I was the intended target."

He thought of the other vampiress lying on the floor. "Did you see who did the shooting?"

She shook her head. "Male, human. But he was already up the stairs and gone before anyone could react."

Trevor frowned. "That's odd. How could a human escape a room full of vampires?"

"How indeed." She raised one elegant eyebrow. "I recognize you. You have been to my show?"

He nodded. "Twice."

Her full mouth twitched up at the corners into a warm smile. "I like repeat customers."

"Your voice is amazing."

"What is your name?"

"Trevor Blackstone."

She eyed him curiously. "Hmm, Blackstone. You come from an old witch family. I may have known your ancestors."

Although he had lived most of his life in Nouveau Monde, it still rattled him a little when he met people who knew his grandmother or great-grandfather. People who looked as young as he was.

She brought her long slim hand up to the zipper on the side of her gown intending to pull it down so Trevor could get at the bullet hole, but her hand stilled, and he got the sense that she was listening to something out of his hearing range.

"What is it?" he asked.

It was then that he heard gunshots from beyond the door.

"What the hell?" Trevor rushed to the door to open it. But it was still locked. He glanced over his shoulder to Guinevere. "Open it."

"I can't. It has a failsafe for my protection."

"So we're trapped in this room?"

She shook her head. "No. There is another way out." She pointed to the giant hearth in the corner where a fire raged on. "Through the fire, is a latch. Pull it and a secret door will open."

Trevor looked into the hearth searching for the latch. "We need to douse these flames."

"It's magic and can't be put out with water. "

Without another thought, Trevor reached through the fire and grabbed the latch. He didn't feel the flames. They didn't touch his skin. He was blessed with healing hands, a gift that accompanied his witch genes. They were part of what made him a good EMT.

He pulled the lever. A small trap door opened in the marble floor in front of the fireplace under Trevor's foot. He toppled forward. Guinevere was quick and grabbed him by the jacket before he went down into the hole. Yanking him back, she managed to rip the material from its lining.

He nodded to her. "Thanks."

"No problem."

He motioned toward the trap door. Guinevere stepped into the hole and onto a metal ladder. She climbed down. Trevor waited until the top of her head was out of sight, then followed her. He closed the trap door and plunged them into total darkness.

"Damn it," Trevor swore. He had not anticipated the total lack of light.

"Don't worry, I can see in the dark." She patted him lightly on the leg in reassurance. "I will guide the way."

Trevor held on tightly to the ladder, as he continued his descent.

"I've reached the bottom," Guinevere announced. "Three more rungs and so will you."

He stepped down onto solid ground and felt Guinevere beside him. Her eyes glowed yellow as she looked at him. Grabbing his hand, she pulled him forward into the dark.

"It's a tunnel. It will lead us to a storm drain that empties into the river."

"There're no rats in here, are there?"

Guinevere chuckled. "Are you afraid of them?"

Trevor shook his head, then wondered if she could see the action. "No, not really. I just don't want to catch some disease while I'm walking through the pitch black."

She tugged him further into the tunnel. He had to trust her that she wasn't leading him astray, or into something that could injure him.

"What was all that, anyway?"

"What do you mean?"

"The gunshots?" he asked. "It didn't seem like it was random. A gunman doesn't come back if it's not personal."

He heard her sigh and wondered if she was going to tell him the truth. Not that she was required to. He wasn't anyone to her. Just an EMT in the wrong place at the wrong time.

"It seems I'm involved in a bit of a political war."

"A turf war?"

She sighed again. "I suppose you could call it that. I have control over certain parts of Nouveau Monde, certain businesses and whatnot. My second, Soren, has chosen to move against me."

"So this was an assassination attempt on your life?" Trevor was surprised. He knew about vampire politics, but didn't think it involved mafia-like tactics. He'd never heard of one vampire moving on another like this.

"Yes, I suppose it was."

Trevor was silent the rest of the way as Guinevere guided him through the tunnel. Of course, he didn't have a choice. It was completely black. He couldn't see a thing except for the eerie amber glow of Guinevere's eyes when she turned to check on his progress.

Eventually, Trevor could see a small pinpoint of light. They were nearing the end of the tunnel. Cold water sloshed around his feet, sending shivers up his legs. They were obviously in the storm drain.

Guinevere slowed. She tightened the hold on his hand.

"What's wrong?"

"I'm not sure."

He could feel the shivers wracking her body. He didn't think vampires got cold, but maybe she hadn't ingested any blood recently and she was reacting to the loss of heat in her limbs.

"Have you fed lately?"

"No, not since before the show."

According to Trevor's calculations that would've been over six hours ago. Guinevere definitely needed blood especially since she'd lost some from being shot.

The light became larger as they neared the drain's exit. Trevor could hear the rush of the river beyond them. He hoped there was a way out of the drain other than jumping into the river.

As they approached the drain cover, Guinevere crouched down to peer out. Trevor did the same. In the pale moonlight, he could see that her face was drawn and her eyes had darkened. She was in significant pain. Maybe the bullet had fragmented inside her. If there was even the tiniest piece of silver in her bloodstream it could slowly poison her.

"I need to look at your wound, and treat it now. I think you're going into shock."

"We don't have time. We have to get out of this tunnel and to a safe place."

"If I don't treat you now, you'll die." He knew he sounded brusque, but he didn't want to waste time explaining. He knew she wouldn't listen. Guinevere was a woman accustomed to giving orders and expecting them to be followed immediately. But Trevor wasn't one of her minions or employees. He was the guy who was going to save her life.

CHAPTER TWO

SHE LOOKED AT Trevor for what seemed like an eternity, but was really only a second or two. Her gaze was intense and it seemed to pierce him right through, making him feel open and vulnerable. Over the years he'd treated hundreds of vampires, lycans and witches in the city of Nouveau Monde but he'd never been around an Otherworld creature as potent as Mistress Guinevere was.

Standing, she reached up to the zipper on her gown and slid it down her side, over her hip, and letting it pool at her feet, she stepped out of it. Underneath she wore a bra and tiny panties.

He knelt to inspect her wound. Because of the inadequate light, he had to press his face close to her side just underneath the band of her bra. The wound had closed up some, a testament to the healing powers of vampires, and to his healing ability, but it appeared swollen and off color. It was definitely silver infected.

"I have to open it again. It's infected."

He glanced up at her. She nodded for him to go ahead.

Trevor opened his kit and took out his scalpel. It was standard issue for an EMT in Nouveau Monde for exactly situations like this. He poised the tip of the blade above the wound.

"This is going to hurt."

"I have endured worse."

As quick as he could, he sliced the wound open. She winced but didn't move as he dug into the hole with a pair of forceps looking for the piece of silver that had to be inside.

He grimaced as he worked, knowing he was inflicting pain on Guinevere.

After another few seconds of poking and prodding, he found the offending shard and extracted it from her flesh. It was the size of a grain of rice, but had the ability to kill her.

He tossed the piece to the ground then set about closing up her wound again. He gently placed the palm of his right hand over her wound. Closing his eyes, he concentrated and forced all his healing powers through his hand and into her.

As he worked, Guinevere sucked in a breath and reached out to grab his head. She wrapped her fingers in his hair and pulled as his power stitched up her flesh and skin.

"Oh good Lord," she muttered under her breath.

When he was finished, Trevor pulled his hand back and stood. The skin on his palm tingled like pins and needles. It didn't normally feel like that.

"Are you okay?" he asked.

Her eyes were closed and she was bracing her other hand against the side of the tunnel to keep her balance. Slowly she opened her eyes and pinned him with her fierce gaze. Her eyes looked black. "I've never felt anything like that before."

"I'm sorry if I hurt you."

She smiled. "That was not pain I was feeling."

"Oh." He could feel his face flush and he dropped his gaze.

"You have an incredible power, Trevor."

"Should I help you with your dress after I bandage you?"

She shook her head. "No. It's too binding."

"Aren't you cold?" He couldn't help his gaze from traveling over her svelte form. She was incredible to look at.

"I don't feel the temperature."

Trevor bent down to return the scalpel and forceps and to retrieve the bandages and tape from his kit. As quick as he could, he covered up her side. Then he stripped off his jacket, handing it to her.

"Here, just in case you get cold."

She looked at the offered jacket and back at him. "Thank you for the gesture." She took it and put it on.

"Now what?" He looked toward the drain cover. "Out into the river?"

Guinevere followed his gaze and nodded. "That is the only exit."

He reached for the cover and pushed it out. There was a telltale splash as it hit the water. He poked his head out to survey the situation.

But she grabbed him and pulled him back in. "Someone is out there."

Surprised, he scanned the river shore. "I don't see anyone."

"There're two men beside the small clump of trees."

Trevor squinted out into the night, searching the shoreline. He saw nothing. No, wait— he did see a dark shape beside the trees. The shape moved.

"How many people know about this tunnel?"

"Five including myself."

"Could be just kids making out."

Guinevere smiled grimly. "Kids carrying rifles?"

"You can see that?"

She nodded. He guessed he shouldn't be that surprised. Vampires had far superior eyesight and hearing.

"What's the plan then?"

"We jump and try not to get shot."

Guinevere kicked off her shoes. Trevor watched, enthralled by her movements in the moonlight. After she was done, he continued to stare at her long shapely legs, and the point of their juncture. Everything she did was fluid and graceful, like watching a cat slink across the room.She was mesmerizing.

Guinevere slapped him hard across the face.

Trevor shook his head, shocked from the force of the blow. His eyes narrowed as he glared at her. "What was that for?"

"You're not focused. You're going to get hurt if you can't think straight."

He rubbed his stinging cheek. She was right. He had to get his head together. Thinking about touching her skin again was not going to get them safely out of here.

"I'll go first. The men will likely start shooting, then you dive into the water and swim to the far shore." Her eyes narrowed at him. "You can swim, I hope?"

"Yeah, I can swim."

"Okay. We will meet back on shore." She leaned forward and pressed her lips to his cheek. A tiny spark sizzled over his skin where she touched him. "Good luck."

Without another word, she turned and jumped out of the tunnel. The sound of gunfire wasn't far behind her.

Trevor leaned out and watched her hit the water, hopefully unscathed. Taking a deep breath, he flung himself out of the drain, diving into the river.

The moment he hit the water, Trevor lost all the air in his lungs. The bitter icy grip of the water squeezed the warmth from him. Almost instantly his body started to shut down.

He opened his eyes but saw nothing. It was black as the night. He was disoriented and in shock. He had no idea which way Guinevere had swum. He could do nothing but go up, and hope like hell that a bullet didn't slam into his frozen head. He wouldn't heal like the vampiress. The bullet whether it was lead or silver would kill him.

He swam to the surface and broke water. No bullets. So far so good. He was not far from the shore. Trevor had to get out of the water. It was too cold. He would get hypothermia before long, then he'd just be a floating target.

There was no noticeable movement on shore. He swam and crawled out onto the grass. He lay on his back to catch his breath. Already he was shivering. Before long he wouldn't be able to move. He rolled over onto his side and gained his hands and knees.

That was when he heard the distinctive sound of a round going into a chamber.

"Don't move."

"I'm a medical technician. I'm not a vampire. I was responding to a call at the Sinsational club and got trapped. I'm just trying to get back to the hospital."

"Shut up!" The man brought his gun down on Trevor's back. He collapsed on the grass, a stinging pain vibrating up and down his spine.

"Hey, Chuck! I found…"

Trevor felt drops of something hit the side of his cheek. It ran down into his mouth. Blood. His stomach rolled over and bile rose to his throat as he looked up at his assailant.

Rivulets of blood were quickly running from the man's open mouth. His eyes rolled back into his head and he fell sideways. Behind him, Guinevere stood wet and wild-eyed, her hand covered in blood and gore.

She bent down and grabbed Trevor's arm. She yanked him roughly to his feet. "Can you run? We need to escape. I can sense Soren is near, searching the water for me."

He nodded, not able to find his voice.

"I could carry you."

"No," he stuttered. "I can manage." Trevor didn't have an ego, but he did possess some male pride. And being carried by a woman, a vampiress yet, to safety wasn't his idea of dignified.

She grabbed his hand and they ran from the river and into the trees.

CHAPTER THREE

THEY MANAGED to stumble downtown, hiding in the alleys and cautious with every movement they made. Guinevere had expected Trevor to go his own way but he'd promised to get her someplace safe first. His instincts were to heal. She liked that about him. She didn't normally have that type of man in her life. Most were born dominators, killers to be blunt. It was just ingrained in a vampire's genetics to hunt and seek blood. Lycans too for that matter.

Witches on the other hand were all about seeking solace. She needed that in her life. She'd gone too long in a state of paranoia and defense. Constantly watching her back. It was getting tedious and bothersome.

As they ducked down another back alley, she noticed a sign for a cheap ratty hotel called Blue Moon. It was probably run by lycans but she couldn't be choosy right now. She just needed to get indoors to rest and regroup. She also needed to feed. Besides, it would be dawn soon. Although she could face the sun—most vampires could nowadays—she preferred to be under roof when the sun broke the dark sky. Being hungry and hot wasn't a good combination.

"Do you have any money?" she asked him.

He nodded. "I always keep about fifty Euros in my kit for emergencies."

"A room should cost about that. I'll pay you back."

He looked at her with a frown. "Don't worry about it. Let's just get you inside and safe."

The lycan manning the front desk barely batted an eye at her and Trevor as they came in and paid for a room. She supposed he'd seen much worse than a witch in an EMT uniform and a vampiress in nothing but a bra and panties. It brought a whole new meaning to sexual role playing.

The room was what she expected for forty Euros. It was at least clean. She didn't smell any horribly offending odors when they entered, just the usual bleach and faint body sweat.

Trevor helped her to the bed although he was the one shivering from the cold. His clothes were soaked.

"You should get dry or you'll get sick," she suggested

as she lay down on her back on the bed. She needed rest. Her body was barely hanging on.

He nodded. "Let's get you settled, then I will figure something out." He went over to her to inspect her bandages. "You should let me call someone. My friends in law enforcement can help you. Protect you."

She shook her head. "Vampire politics and law enforcement do not mix well. Besides, I don't trust easily. My enemies could have moles inside the department."

"You're trusting me." He met her gaze and held it as he unwrapped her bandage to inspect her wound.

He had amazing hazel eyes with flecks of green. Warm and inviting. She knew the second she met him that she could trust him. That was why she'd beckoned him into her private room to help her with her injuries. He had a protector aura about him. Which was probably why he'd chosen his particular profession.

"You have a trustworthy look about you."

He smiled, as he pressed his fingers to her skin around her bullet wound. The heat of his fingertips sent a wave of pleasure through her. She suspected it was more than just his healing powers that she was reacting to.

Trevor was an attractive man, with unkempt light brown hair and crinkles at his eyes when he smiled. It made a woman want to run her hands through his hair and kiss those laugh lines.

"The wound looks good. It's healing well." He reached

for new bandages in his kit, which he'd kept through the ordeal in the river by strapping it onto his back.

She sat up so he could tape her up again. As he wrapped the gauze around her torso, Guinevere inhaled his scent. It was a mixture of wet male and nature. It was a clean smell like spring rain. It was a good smell. One that made her feel comfortable and secure.

He must've sensed that she was testing him because after affixing the tape securely he pulled back and distanced himself across the room. "It should be all healed in a couple of days. You might have a scar though."

"It's of no consequence. I have others." She stretched out her arms, fully aware that the movement enhanced her bustline. "I wanted to thank you for saving my life. And for getting me here to safety. You didn't have to."

He avoided looking at her, but she could tell he was intrigued by her. Interested maybe. "Anyone would have done the same thing."

She shook her head. "I suspect that you are just not anyone."

He fussed with his medical kit. "Is there anything else I can do for you before I go?"

She wondered what he would do if she told him straight out what she wanted from him. Would he run if he knew how much she desired him right now?

He looked over at her, his eyes darkening. Did he sense what she needed?

"I need to feed, Trevor." Her hands were shaking. She

pressed them against the bed, hoping he did not see how much she craved him.

"I saw a vending machine in the lobby, I can get you a couple of bottles of blood. What do you prefer?"

"That will not be enough. I need fresh warm blood or I will not heal properly."

She saw him swallow. Would he make his escape now knowing what she asked of him?

"Do you have a regular donor you could call? I could go down to the street and see if I could find you a willing one."

She shook her head. "There is no one. No one I can trust."

His hands paused on his medical bag. She could see his indecision in them. "I'm not sure—"

Guinevere rose from the bed and crossed the room. She stopped a foot in front of him, not wanting to scare him away. She needed him to breach the small distance between them. She needed him to agree to what she asked. She'd never taken anyone against their will before, and she wasn't about to start now.

Even when she'd first risen as a vampire, some eight hundred years ago, she'd been careful who she took blood from. She'd never forcibly bitten someone. It had always been consensual. At first she'd had to seduce her donors but now in these enlightened times, she'd only have to ask. Most people understood the pleasure of a vampire's bite. And most of them craved it just as much as she, like a drug.

"Have you shared blood with a vampire before?"

He shook his head.

"I won't hurt you."

"I know."

Narrowing her eyes, she studied him. "Do you not find me attractive?"

"I do, yes."

"But?"

He sighed. "I don't want to take advantage of you. You're hurt and—"

"You are afraid of taking advantage of me?" She laughed.

Her laughter made him frown. "I don't take my healing oaths lightly, Guinevere, and neither should you."

She sobered and really looked at him. She'd never met a stronger man before. A more valiant man. It was a trait she didn't often see in people, especially those who surrounded her, those who ran in her political circles.

This just made her want him that much more.

"I did not mean to offend you. That wasn't my intention."

He nodded that he accepted her apology. "Look, I'm sure I can find you someone to feed from." He turned toward the door. "It won't take long."

She grabbed his arm. "I don't want someone else, I want you."

"It's the situation talking. We were in a dangerous, life-threatening situation together. We've bonded because of it."

She knew he was trying to work out the particulars in his mind, trying to find reasons why they shouldn't succumb to the desire she could feel simmering in the air. It was a human thing.

"Does it matter, Trevor? I want you, and I know you want me. I can see it in the way you look at me and the way your heart speeds up when you touch me."

He didn't say anything right away and Guinevere took that as a sign that he was considering her words carefully. There was no denying his desire for her. She could see it in his eyes and read it in the way he responded to her.

She didn't normally, but she closed the distance between them and wrapped a hand around his neck to bring his mouth to hers. He didn't resist her. Then finally, they were kissing, and it was hard and hot and wet and everything she was hoping it would be.

He wrapped his arms around her, and bending her back, he deepened the kiss. He was urgent, all tongue and teeth. He nipped and tugged at her lips and seemingly drank her in. It was as if he too was starving, and the only thing to sate him was her.

CHAPTER FOUR

THE VERY LAST THING Trevor expected to be doing when he woke up this morning was kissing a gorgeous eight-hundred-year-old vampiress. Pulling bullets out of her maybe, but definitely not making out with her.

He'd had vampire girlfriends in the past, there was just something about vampires he was drawn to, but none were as powerful or as seductive as Guinevere. She stood out above them all.He pressed his hands along her back as he moved his mouth over hers and down over her chin to her neck, teasing her, tasting her. She tasted exotic, an unusual mixture of lemon and spices. Not what he expected considering her Celtic coloring and the lilt in her voice. It was the taste of a woman who was steeped in ancient history and who had traveled many years across the world and back. She seemed to carry the flavor of several cultures on her skin like a perfume.

He trailed his tongue along her throat and up to her ear, lightly sucking on her lobe. She moaned against him, her hands making small work of his uniform shirt. She had it off him in seconds and tossed it, still damp, onto the floor.

She ran her hands over his chest and he found he couldn't contain his groan of pleasure at the way she touched him. Soft yet possessive. As if she'd not touched a man in a long time.

"We don't have to have sex, if you don't want to," she murmured against his mouth. "I could just take blood."

"No, I definitely want to."

She laughed and the sound was so sexy it made him hard.

Still peppering kisses to her lips, to her neck, cheek and mouth, he backed her up to the bed. Once the mattress hit the back of her knees, she went down, pulling him with her.

She lay on her back, and Trevor covered her with his body. He hovered over her, his arms braced against the mattress. He didn't want to injure her further. She still needed to heal. Although by the way she yanked him down, he didn't think she was feeling any discomfort or pain.

He kissed her mouth, then moved down to her shoulder, lavishing attention to her collarbone then over to her other shoulder. She gave him a sly look when he ventured lower, trailing his tongue over the swell of her perfect pale breasts.

"It unhooks in the front," she breathed.

Trevor flicked the clasp open and looked his fill of her. She was flawless in every way. Pale round breasts with rose-tipped nipples beckoned him to feel and to taste. He did both.

He sucked one pebbled nub into his mouth and rolled it around on his tongue, pulling and suckling at will. Guinevere bowed her back and wrapped a hand in his hair to urge him on. He didn't disappoint, and bestowed the same attention to her other nipple, applying both tongue and teeth until she was a whimpering writhing pool on the bed.

He moved down her torso, mindful of her bandages, and pressed his lips to her belly, circling her navel with the tip of his tongue. Then he ventured lower still.

Hooking his fingers into the thin band of her panties, he pulled them down the long length of her legs. He tossed the garment to the side and settled himself between her legs. He trailed one finger around her belly then over the light sprinkling of red hair on her mound. Then sliding his hand down, he slipped into her hot silk center and prepared to worship her completely.

Guinevere's breath hitched in her throat, as his fingers

brushed over her sensitive flesh again and again. Like a gentle breeze, his hands swept over her, careful not to touch too much too soon. He was teasing her, and it was driving her insane.

The throb at her center intensified, hovering close to the line between pleasure and pain. She needed to feed. The hunger clawed at her, but this pleasure was too much to forgo. She wanted him in any way he was willing to give her.

Her wishes did not go long unfulfilled. Lying down on his stomach between her spread legs, Trevor parted her with his thumbs. She could feel his hot breath on her intimate flesh as he nuzzled his face into her. Lightly at first, he trailed his tongue up and down, swirling the tip as he reached her opening.

Heaving, Guinevere thrashed about on the mattress. The torment of his tongue sent her spiraling under waves of pleasure. Each time he neared the throbbing nerves, she thought she'd die from the agony of near release. She moaned urgently to him.

As if bowing to her wishes, Trevor nudged her flesh with the tip of his tongue. She jerked up in response to the hot lash of pleasure that whipped over her. With one hand, he pressed on her belly, keeping her still while he continued his delicious assault on her flesh. He lapped at her slick core, concentrating on her most sensitive spot, suckling on it between strokes of his tongue.

With ease, he slid two fingers into her. She could feel him pressing against her delicate flesh, as if searching for just the right spot. She prayed he'd find it soon and end her agony.

The heat between her thighs was building, nearing unbearable. Guinevere was close to climaxing. The muscles in her belly and thighs tightened, preparing her for the overwhelming rush of ecstasy. A few more flicks of Trevor's talented tongue, and she'd dive over the edge.

As he continued to thrust his fingers in and out, pushing as deep as he could go, he suckled on her. She could feel his teeth scrape against her sensitive flesh as he sucked on her and she cried out from the delight of it.

With one final lunge of his hand, she orgasmed hard. Clamping her eyes shut against the sudden rush of pleasure, she screamed as he found her spot. He pressed hard just as he clamped down on her wet core with his lips.

She came in a hot blinding rush. She couldn't get her breath. Thrashing about, she grabbed onto Trevor's head, pulling on his hair, but he remained affixed to her. He continued to lick and suckle her, prolonging her orgasm.

Another powerful jolt of ecstasy zinged over her. Again, her body tightened and writhed on the bed. Sizzling hot flicks of pleasure assaulted her body one right after another, until she could not think beyond the sensations deep inside her body.

And that was when her hunger broke free from its bonds and forced her to act.

She bolted up, and grabbing Trevor she spun him around to the side of the bed, so that he was sitting up near the edge and she was pressed intimately into his back. She wrapped her arms around his chest, and nuzzled her face into the crook of his neck. He smelled so damn good she could barely contain herself.

She could feel the quivers in his body and smell the excitement and the fear rushing through his veins. Both scents drove her forward. She liked that he wanted it.

"Have you ever been bitten before?" she whispered into his ear.

He shook his head. "I've never been tempted before now."

"Once I bite you, you'll crave it afterwards. You'll crave me. Can you live with that?"

He nodded.

Guinevere kissed the side of his neck. She laved her tongue over his skin, sucking and nipping playfully. He moaned loudly when she scraped the tips of her fangs over his vein. It wouldn't take much to puncture his skin. But she knew how to make it easy, how to make it hot.

A vampire could make the bite hurt or make it feel so damn good, like a drug rush going straight to all the erogenous zones. She could make Trevor so hard with her bite that he'd scream in both pleasure and agony.

Tilting his head to the side, she settled her mouth over his flesh. With her other hand she reached down and found the hot hard length of him still imprisoned in his pants. She cupped him, feeling him grow ever harder in her palm. He was ready.

Baring her fangs, she lifted up then sank them into Trevor's neck. She moaned as an explosion of flavor erupted in her mouth as his sweet blood rushed in. She swallowed a mouthful, mindful to not take too much this first time.

A surge of hot searing pleasure pierced her body and she nearly gasped from the shock of it. She'd never experienced pure euphoria before drinking blood.

So, she closed her eyes and reveled in it.

CHAPTER FIVE

TREVOR BOWED his back as a fusion of pain and pleasure shot through his body. The second Guinevere's fangs pierced his skin he knew he was in for an experience beyond anything he'd ever felt.

Every suck on his neck drew a line right down to his groin. He squeezed his eyes shut against the pressure between his legs. He'd never been as hard as he was right now. It was almost painful.

He struggled against the sensations coursing through him, but she held him firm with her hands and her mouth. Damn, he knew vampires were strong, but the immensity of her strength jolted him.

As she continued to draw his blood from his neck, she massaged him through his pants with her hand. Barely holding onto his thoughts, he unbuttoned his pants to allow her free access. She took it immediately and her long slim hand blissfully wrapped around his girth.

While her lips and teeth stroked his flesh around his throat, her hand stroked his cock. At first it was long and slow. A languid torturous pace. Then she picked up the momentum and Trevor found he was barely holding on to his sanity.

He didn't want to orgasm like this, he wanted to be inside her when he did. He wanted to bury himself so deep that he wouldn't be able to tell where he ended and she started. The urge was so intense it made his teeth ache and his bones throb.

He grabbed her hand to still her. "Stop," he panted, hardly able to form coherent words. "Not like this."

She paused, then he heard the sound of her mouth coming off his flesh. The sound was audible, like a suction cup coming off tile. "What's wrong?" She was as breathless as he.

He could feel twin rivulets of warm blood coursing down his chest and his back.

"I want to be inside you when I come."

Without a word, she stepped off the bed, helped him off with his pants, and with him still sitting, she straddled his lap. She reached down between them, gripped him firmly in her hand and slowly lowered herself until she was fully seated.

Trevor bit down on his lip, breaking skin as she settled

smoothly on him. She felt so damn good he could barely function. He slid his hands down her back to grip her firm rear end. Holding her tight, he helped her move up and down, searching for that perfect rhythm that would drive them both mad.

As Guinevere rode him, she found his mouth with hers. They kissed as if both desperate for air, as if the only oxygen available was within each other. She nipped and tugged at his lips. He was completely aware that she licked at the blood on his mouth from his bitten lip. He liked that. That she consumed all of him.

He was at her mercy. She could do what she wanted to him and he'd welcome it.

They kissed again. He lifted his hips to meet her as he pulled her down. The movement caused him to bury himself deep inside her. He grunted against her lips from the effort and from the intensity that was building inside him. He wasn't going to be able to hold on for much longer.

Guinevere wrapped her arms around Trevor's neck as she rocked on him. She buried her face in his neck, licking at the bite marks to close them up. The blood was slowing because of her saliva which had coagulating qualities to it. She'd taken enough from him. Although she could've feasted on him all night. His blood tasted like ambrosia. She'd never sampled something so delectable before.

But now his blood was racing through her. She could feel it mingling with her own. It contained power, that was certain. Like electricity, it sizzled along her veins making all her muscles and flesh quiver deliciously.

Although she'd told him that he would crave her bite from this day forward, what she wouldn't tell him, what she would never admit, was that she knew she would crave him as well. This male witch was addicting to be sure. And it wasn't just his blood she desired, but all of him as well.

She dug her nails into his back as he drove her up. He was stronger than he looked. His arms and chest were roped with muscle so when he wrapped his arms around her and pulled her, it was nice and tight and secure. She felt safe pressed against him.

No other man before him had ever made her feel like she wanted or needed to be protected. She'd been on top for so long, the one in charge, the boss, that she'd long forgotten what it was like to feel safeguarded from all harm in a man's arms.

It was that thought that she clung to as she closed her eyes and came in a maddening hot rush. Trevor squeezed her tighter and with a loud moan he came just as hard.

They held each other for another few minutes as they gathered their senses and learned how to breathe properly again. Guinevere opened her eyes and looked down into his face.

He smiled at her, sweat slicking his forehead and top lip. His hair was wet and she ran her fingers through it playfully. Leaning down, she pressed her lips to his. She kissed him gently, but then he wrapped a hand around the back of her neck and deepened the kiss until they both lost their breath once more.

When they broke apart, Guinevere slowly unhooked her leg from around his waist and rolled onto the mattress onto her back. He turned and lay on his side next to her. He played his fingers along her rib cage.

"You're almost healed."

She half smiled, still feeling lazy and sex-drugged. "That is your amazing blood at work."

He leaned down and pressed a kiss to just below her bandage. "You're amazing."

Guinevere glanced at the curtained window. She could feel dawn nearing. She turned and looked Trevor deep in the eyes, feeling vulnerable again. "Will you hold me until I sleep?"

He nodded, then snuggled up along her side. Smiling, Guinevere rolled onto her good side, and grabbing his hand, pulled his arm over her. He nestled into her back and pressed a kiss to her shoulder blade.

"Thank you," she murmured.

"You're most welcome."

She closed her eyes, and let her body relax. It was easy to do with Trevor so close, holding her, stroking a hand up and down her hip. She hadn't felt this contented in more years than she could remember. Maybe never since becoming a vampire. And that was a long time ago.

She knew it was a lot to ask, but she hoped that he was still there, snuggled with her when she woke again. She'd like to continue their, whatever it seemed to be, liaison further if he wanted to. And for the first time she was afraid that he would say no and she'd be alone again.

CHAPTER SIX

THE SUN wasn't quite down all the way when Guinevere woke. But she sensed it was close enough. Blinking open her eyes, she stared at the grungy hotel room wall she was facing, trying to piece the last twelve hours together in her mind.

One of the first things she noticed was that she was under the covers. Sometime while she slept Trevor must've put the blanket over top of her. The second thing she noticed was that she was alone.

She rolled over onto her other side and stared at Trevor's space on the bed and at the empty room. She'd hoped he'd stay, but she didn't expect it. He'd done more than was necessary for her. Healing her, getting her to a safe place. What had she been expecting? That he'd fallen in love with her and couldn't leave her? It was ridiculous to even harbor such thoughts.

She sat up and stretched. Her body felt good as new, better even from ingesting Trevor's witch blood. Her finger played over the bandage around her ribs and she tore it off. She tossed the soiled gauze away and looked down to inspect her side.

Her skin was smooth and unmarked. It was as if she'd never been shot. If it wasn't for the slight raise of her flesh that she felt with her index finger she couldn't have even noticed any difference. Beyond that, there was no visual evidence that she'd ever been hurt. It was amazing even to a vampiress as experienced as she.

Trevor's blood was beyond anything she'd come across. She'd only drunk a little and he'd completely healed her of an infected bullet wound. She could only imagine what it could do if she'd taken even more. She thought he should bottle it and sell it. He'd make a billion on his medicinal essence.

Smiling, she pushed off the blanket and redressed in her bra and panties. She noticed Trevor's jacket then, hanging on the back of the only chair, and she slid it on. Had he forgotten it in his haste to leave or had he deliberately left it for her? She liked to think it was the latter.

At least she was partially clothed for the things she had to do next. She had several calls she needed to make and since she didn't have her cell phone, she had to go down to the lobby and find a land phone. Her staff needed to be contacted. She wanted to make sure they were safe and unharmed. And she also needed to secure her own safety. The only way she could do that was by surrounding herself with people she could trust. Unfortunately, she was starting to doubt that those people existed in her life.

It was clear that Soren would not stop until she was dead. And he would use whatever means were at his disposal to achieve his goal. He was obviously using someone close to her or she would never have been attacked at Sinsational. Her club had been her sanctuary, or so she thought. She had believed it to be the one place she could feel secure. She'd been wrong.

If it hadn't been for Trevor…

She pushed thoughts of him from her mind. She hadn't mooned over a man in many years, and she wasn't going to start now. She had work to do and little time to do it.

Trevor balanced the two scalding hot coffees and bag of croissants as he mounted the stairs to the third-floor hotel room. He checked his watch. It was past seven at night and he figured Guinevere would be rising soon. For some corny reason he wanted to be there when she woke.

He'd woken up over an hour ago and had snuck out to get some coffee and food for them both, and he'd also wanted to call his friend, Inspector Bellmonte, about the shooting. They hadn't arrested anyone, and were still searching for suspects. Trevor told him what Guinevere had said about her partner, Soren. Gabriel had taken it under advisement. And then asked whether Guinevere would be willing to go on record.

Trevor confessed that he had doubted it. He knew Guinevere had refused any type of police protection, but Trevor felt that she might need it in the end. So he had discussed it with Gabriel. It would be there, if she wanted it. Now, he just had to convince her that she needed it.

As he walked the hall to the room, he wondered why he cared so much. He'd treated hundreds of people, vampires, lycans, witches and humans over the past five years and had never gotten involved. Why now?

It had been the first time he'd been involved in an actual chase, but it had been the second time he'd had a gun to his head. He'd been around the violence of the city all his life, so it wasn't that it was a brand-new experience to him.

It was Guinevere that made the difference.

He was drawn to her. He felt her need for him. She was one of the strongest, most powerful vampiresses in the city, and Trevor sensed she needed him. That she'd felt comfortable and secure with him. It was a good feeling to be needed by such an enthralling woman. And the sex had been spectacular. He'd never come that hard in his life.

Did he think it would go beyond their brief tryst? Not

really. Did he want it to? That was the million-dollar question. And he wasn't sure if he had any answer to it.

He put his hand on the door to open it, but paused. He sensed something was amiss. He took his hand from the doorknob and pressed his ear to the door. His hearing wasn't like a vampire's or a lycan's but he'd trained himself to really listen. He could hear things that most humans couldn't.

And he heard some of those things inside the room.

He could hear Guinevere breathing, but it wasn't normal. It was labored. Something or someone was causing undue stress to her body. He guessed it was a someone. She must've woken and called her people.

Maybe Soren had shown up instead.

Trevor looked down at himself. He wasn't prepared to take on a vampire of what he could only guess would be Soren's power. If the vampire had been Guinevere's second then he had to possess many superior qualities. Strength being one of them.

But he had to do something. He couldn't just stand here like an idiot with hot coffee in one hand and a bag of rolls in the other. Wait. Didn't he have something in his medical kit? Juggling the coffee, he reached down and unzipped his bag, rummaging around in it until he found what he was looking for.

He pulled out his hand. In his fingers he held a syringe.

Inside was a powerful sedative that he'd used countless times on rabid lycans and out-of-control vampires.

Palming it, he opened the hotel room door and walked in as if he was just returning from getting coffee and nothing more. "I got you black, because I didn't know if you liked cream and sugar."

Trevor had been right. Someone had Guinevere up against the wall, dangling from it actually, his hand closed around her throat. She was definitely having trouble breathing.

The vampire glared at him in surprise. "Get out! We don't need any room service."

Guinevere looked at him. He could plainly see the pain and the anger in her eyes. Blood streaked the front of her body and dripped from the very tips of her toes to pool on the shaggy rug beneath her. It took all Trevor had, not to rush to her side.

Trevor set the coffee and bag of croissants onto the nearby table. "I'm not looking for trouble."

"Then get out."

He shook his head, taking a step forward. "I'm afraid I can't do that."

The vampire looked at Guinevere and shook his head. "Is this your cavalry? A human?" He sneered. "No wonder you're so weak."

Theintruder had to be Soren. Trevor could see the contempt in his face when he regarded Guinevere.

"You don't mind if I make quick work of him, do you my darling Guin?" Soren released his hold on Guinevere. She slumped to the floor, the mass of her red hair falling over her face and chest as she dropped. Like lightning he was across the room in a millisecond, crushing Trevor's windpipe with his hand.

Trevor's lungs deflated losing air instantly. His first instinct was to claw at the vampire's hand, but then he remembered what he held cradled in his palm. And instead, he flipped the cap off with his thumb and plunged the needle into Soren's chest, right into his heart.

Surprised, the vampire looked down at the syringe protruding from his chest. "What's this?" With his free hand, he reached for it, pulled it out and tossed it to the floor. "You're more stupid than I first thought."

Soren squeezed Trevor's throat tighter. Black spots formed in Trevor's vision. It wouldn't be long before he passed out. He knew exactly how long a person could go without oxygen. It wasn't long at all. Human life was so precarious. It could be ended in a second.

And he wondered if he was finally going to understand that fully and not just see it on a day-to-day basis.

Soren's smile began to fade. His brow furrowed and he narrowed his eyes. He started to lick his lips. Trevor knew that his face was going numb. The sedative was kicking in. But would it be fast enough? Trevor wasn't sure he had any more than a minute left before he was done.

Before Trevor could kick out one last time against the agony of suffocating, Soren was flying across the room. He hit the far wall, and fell to the floor, unconscious. Guinevere grabbed Trevor right before he could collapse.

She lowered him to the ground, and brushed a hand over his face. She shook her head. "What were you thinking?"

He could barely understand her. Her words were jumbled together and her voice was so hoarse, nearly unrecognizable. It was then that he noticed that most of her throat was torn open.

Lifting his hand he touched her on the neck, on the side that wasn't mangled. He licked his lips, trying to form words around his bruised vocal cords. "You're hurt."

"It'll heal."

He really looked at the gaping wound. He had his doubts it would heal properly. The damage was too immense. She could heal it over time, she wouldn't die, but she'd never be the same. She'd never be able to sing again.

"I can heal you faster." He pulled at his shirt to reveal the bite marks she'd left on his lower neck.

She looked at them, then shook her head. "I've taken too much from you."

"I wouldn't offer if I didn't want to."

She looked him in the eye, to let him know the gravity

of what he offered her. "If I bite you again, it will bind us further."

He nodded. "Yeah, I realize that."

"We hardly know each other."

"I know enough that I want to know you more." He smiled. "Is that okay?"

"It is more than okay."

Trevor sat up straighter and pulled off his shirt. On her knees in front of him, Guinevere leaned forward and settled her mouth over his bite wounds. He sucked in a breath as she buried her fangs into him again.

Her hands slid into his hair as she fed on him. Trevor reached up and grabbed her by the jacket. He had to hold onto something, anything to keep him upright.

It hurt this time. The pain was sharp and searing. It surged down his arms, over his chest, to the very tips of his toes. He gritted his teeth and held on as it took him to a dark place.

Although she didn't feed from him long, it felt like an eternity to Trevor. Even after she removed her teeth from his flesh, he still felt an agonizing throb from his wound. It thumped just as hard as his heart did in his chest.

She leaned back and then touched his face with her fingertips. He met her gaze then lowered to watch in awe as her flesh knitted back together. He'd never seen it go so quickly. It was amazing, even to him, that his blood had that kind of power.

When no more blood seeped from her wound, Guinevere leaned forward and kissed Trevor. "Thank you," she murmured against his lips.

"You're welcome." Then he kissed her back.

And that's how Inspector Gabriel Bellmonte found them in the hotel room when he arrived to arrest Soren for attempted murder and assault.

CHAPTER SEVEN

As GUINEVERE stepped out onto the spotlighted stage, she sensed a difference in this evening's atmosphere It might have been the fact that she hadn't performed in over a month. Since Soren's attack on her, she hadn't been at the club much at all. When she caught the gaze of the man sitting at a table near the stage, she knew exactly why she was feeling so different.

She hadn't seen Trevor since their heated affair in the hotel, but here he was in her club front row and center, and smiling. She returned his smile, then as the white spotlight rose to meet her, she opened her mouth and began to sing, something she never thought to do again after having her throat nearly torn out only thirty days prior.

It was because of him.

After the show, she retired to her private room in the basement of the club. She sat by the fire in the hearth and sipped a glass of red wine. She'd shed her stage clothes in favor of a vibrant red dressing gown. Her feet were bare and curled up under her as she waited. She hoped he didn't make her wait for much longer. The last month had proved difficult without seeing him. She'd never pined for a man, but she definitely had been longing for Trevor.

When the knock came at her door, she smiled, then waved her hand in the air to swing the door open. Trevor stepped inside. The door shut and locked behind him.

Eyebrow raised, he glanced at the door, then back at her. "Am I a prisoner this time?"

"Maybe."

He crossed the room. He didn't sit in the other chair but chose to stand next to her instead. He was close enough that she could touch him if she wanted. She wanted desperately.

"Your show was spectacular as usual."

"Thanks to you." She ran a finger down her throat.

He followed the motion with his eyes. "I'm sorry I—"

She lifted her hand to stop his words. "There's no need to apologize, Trevor. You don't owe me anything."

He licked his lips, then said, "But what if I did want to owe you something? What if I wanted you to be angry that I hadn't come around or called?"

She frowned at him. "You want me to be angry?"

"No, I want you."

"You want me to what?"

He shrugged. "Just, I want you."

Smiling, she stood, so she was mere inches from him. "I want you too."

He reached for her and pulled her to him. Bending her slightly, he covered her mouth with his. He kissed her hard. And it crushed her heart. Everything about Trevor Blackstone was potent.

He nibbled at her lips while he ran his hands up and down her back. "How long until your next show?"

"Hmm, twenty-four hours, give or take."

"Good, that will give me enough time."

"For what?"

"To show you a magic trick."

"What kind of trick?"

He nipped at her earlobe. "The one where I make our clothes disappear for hours and hours."

"Is there a magic word?"

"Maybe."

With a sly grin, Guinevere took a step back, and untied her robe. She let the silky material slide to the floor. "Abracadabra."

Trevor took in her naked form and nodded. "Perfect execution." He grabbed her hand, pulled her to him, and kissed her again.

* * * * *

SALVATION OF
THE DAMNED

Theresa Meyers

CHAPTER ONE

HE'D found her.

At last.

Again.

As if they sensed something dark and extraordinary about him, the costumed party guests separated like water around a ship, allowing Raphael to pass. He barely noticed. All his senses honed in on her evocative scent.

His smile, he knew, would be faintly triumphant as he traced the unique fragrance of night-blooming flowers and hot female flesh that had led him here, to the pulsing heart of New Orleans. For once, he didn't care about showing his fangs or unnatural pallor. The simpletons around him would assume it was only part of a Mardi Gras costume. Foolish mortals. They wouldn't know he was the genuine article until the light in their eyes faded away.

Tonight was not merely a hunt. Tonight was critical to the survival of his kind. The perfume of the woman's blood filled his senses. Despite the hundreds of guests, Raphael separated the light throb of her particular heart-beat from the others. It pulsed, warm and rich, calling to his inner thirst like nothing he had experienced since his turning. His mouth watered, venom flowed and his fangs grew longer in anticipation.

Two days ago her scent had been a mere whisper, a seductive wisp that drifted in on the wind and coiled about his senses. But as the hours slid by, it changed, demanding all his attention, bringing him to her. She drew him, even though he had yet to catch sight of her. He didn't need to see her to know who she was. Put him in a room filled with a thousand women, and her scent alone would identify her as his quarry.

The sacrifice. Their salvation.

Have you found her yet? The voice of the eldest vampire, Janus, the father of them all, intruded into his mind. Urgent. Worried.

Soon.

Be quick. It is nearly time.

I know, I know. I'll have her there by midnight. I always have.

Raphael took a deep breath and flexed his fingers, though it was purely an exercise to calm his mind. He had long since ceased to need his lungs, and the strength in his hands could easily crush a cannon ball.

Her scent grew stronger, filling his nostrils with her enticing heady bouquet, a mixture of jasmine and spiced wine. A taste he hadn't experienced in what felt like forever, yet the memory of the flavor tantalized his tongue. The crowd shifted, exposing a lithe brunette with a stunning profile and lush mouth. Her chocolate-colored hair cascaded loose and free around her creamy shoulders and bare back. Dressed as a Regency-era courtesan in black silk, she captured his attention and that of every man in sight. Laughing, she turned, pale blue eyes sparkling. She was so alive, so vibrant, the very sight of her made his chest ache.

If he still had a beating heart, it would have stopped dead at the sight of her. As it was, a shot of heat that owed nothing to blood flow and everything to raw need, coursed through his body. Only once in six thousand years had he been so affected, and it had cost him dearly. For a thousand years he had mourned that particular woman. Death would have been far easier than living on knowing what he had done.

He couldn't afford to make the same mistake again.

For his kind.

For himself.

She was being watched. Evaline St. Croix sensed the gaze skim down her back like a heated, physical caress.

Casually glancing around at her fellow party guests laughing and dancing around her, she pinpointed the source. A stranger, unlike anyone in her acquaintance. Tall and lean, his eyes covered by a black demi-mask, he moved with a quiet strength and sure grace. His gaze was dark and intense, his thick coffee-colored hair, threaded with strands of gold, brushed the collar of an expensive tuxedo.

Laurie, one of her coworkers at the accounting firm, eyed the stranger, her gaze assessing and hot. "Be still my beating heart." She sounded as breathless as Eva felt. "Please tell me you know Tall, Dark and Dangerous over there. "

No. Yes. She tried not to stare, but everything in Eva wanted to turn and look her fill. "Not sure."

Dragging her gaze away from the stranger striding toward them, the other woman smiled, giving Eva a knowing look. She fanned her face with her hand. "Whew! I feel like a voyeur. I should cover my eyes. My God, he's already undressed you with that smokin' hot look. Any second now, he's going to have you flat on your back in the middle of the dance floor!"

Face hot, Eva's insides tightened in response to the man's ultra-focused attention as he closed the yards between them. It was like being under the bright light of a tractor beam. "Laurie!"

"Well he certainly seems interested in you. Live a little. He could be a lot of fun."

Eva wasn't sure. She threw a quick glance over her shoulder to see who he was looking at with such heat and longing.

"What are you doing?" Laurie demanded, grabbing her arm. "Looking for the exit?"

"Looking to see who he's staring at."

Her friend laughed. "He's looking at *you* like that. Trust me. He only has eyes for you."

He was looking at *her*? Looking at her like she was a supermodel. Eva looked at herself critically in her mirror every morning. Everything was where it was supposed to be. She had nice skin. And her brown hair could be called pretty, well, shiny at least. But she was not, absolutely not, the kind of woman that would make a man like this guy look at her with that level of heat in his gaze.

She'd wanted *something,* Eva thought, a little panicky, and here he was. "Be careful what you wish for," her grandmother used to say. Eva didn't have the kind of imagination that could wish for this man. Not even close. She'd just wanted something—*someone*—to loosen up her straight, and let's face it, rather boring existence. Crunching numbers as a CPA in a cubicle at Cox and Hotchkiss didn't offer much in the way of a good time. She was nothing more than a small, unimportant cog in a big powerful machine. Hardly what she thought her life would amount to, especially considering what she'd already been through.

But who was he? She didn't recall seeing him before, and she knew most of the party guests tonight. They were a mixture of her firm's biggest clients, friends and social acquaintances. A veritable Who's Who of the South.

His lips were definitely kissable. Lips that promised the kind of slow, long, deep kisses that had her fantasizing about all the things his mouth could do. They tipped up slightly in a wicked subtle smile, emphasizing the cleft in his chin as their gazes locked. Dragging her attention away from the faint smile, Eva's gaze clashed with his. Dark topaz eyes, mesmerizing, their message impossible to mistake, held her immobile as party guests swirled around them in a kaleidoscope of color and noise.

Like a work of art, he was too handsome. But it was more than his physical perfection that struck her. Raw primal power radiated from him, causing a ripple in his wake as he moved through the crowded ballroom with an animal grace, cutting through the clusters of guests with ease.

Time suddenly seemed to speed from slow-mo to double time, and in an instant he was right in front of her.

"Would you like to dance?" He held out a broad, smooth hand in invitation. She didn't know him, had never met him, and yet as she stared into the golden liquid depths of his eyes, she felt an instant connection, as if they'd known each other forever.

"Not right now. Thanks." It wasn't just the dance. She sensed that touching him would be the start of something she wasn't going to be able to control. *Walk away from him,* she told herself firmly. Having a fling with any of the firm's clients or their associates would backfire drastically. Her disastrous relationship with Kevin had taught her not to even attend this kind of function.

When it had come to talking about marriage, she'd been honest with him about her past and her destiny. He'd thought she was making up excuses and a bit crazy. In his anger he pulled his multi-million dollar account from the firm, and she'd lost both her job and a measure of her self-confidence. She'd only come tonight because Laurie had assured her Kevin wouldn't be here.

But at the moment, staring into the stranger's eyes, Eva found she didn't give a damn. Her skin grew hot, her knees weak, the longer she gazed at the man before her. It had been far too long since a man had numbed her brain this thoroughly by just being next to her, and it made her head spin.

"It's only a dance."

Walk away. This man is...not like Kevin. She'd had no problem telling Kevin no. She seriously doubted she could do the same with this man. She couldn't form the thought. Despite all her logical mental objections, her body seemed to have a will of its own, and Eva found herself placing her hand in his. The cool firmness of his touch against her skin startled her and sent an electrical current up her arm that was shocking in its intensity. Her fingers automatically tightened in his. How foolish. It was this man she was afraid of, yet it was this man she wanted to cling to.

"Scared?" he taunted lightly, as she resisted the tug of his hand.

"To dance? Not at all." Eva managed a small smile as she flowed into his arms. Her heart pumped so hard that the rush of blood in her ears made it difficult to hear the thumping base in the music. Their steps seemed synchronized as they moved easily together. "I'm Evaline St. Croix," Eva told him with forced lightness. The party, loud and boisterous only moments before, seemed to fall away, leaving just the two of them on the dance floor.

His hand felt cool and dry against hers. He smiled slightly, his golden eyes dancing with humor—and something else Eva couldn't name. Something that made her heart pound even harder and caused her blood to flow hot and fast through her veins. "So what's your name?"

"Raphael," he told her, after several seconds where she suspected he was assessing her in a way no man had ever done before.

His name suited him. "Are you supposed to be a dark angel, then?"

Something deep in his gaze sparkled. "Hardly. It's an old family name."

"My friends call me Eva."

"And what may I call you?"

For a moment, her mouth refused to work as thoughts hit her mind in a rush. *Call me sexy, tempting, anything you want as long as you touch me.*

His mouth twitched, as if she'd said the words out loud rather than thought them, and she swallowed, grateful he couldn't read her mind. She tried to find her voice, but the words came out nearly a whisper. "Eva will do."

At least the dance floor was crowded and the music was fast-paced. That might give her time to rein in her raging libido before she did anything to embarrass herself or her employer.

But her fragile security vanished once the music changed to a slow sultry salsa. Taking her hands, he tugged her close, the heels of his hands resting against her hips. She smelled his intoxicating cologne, and the starch in his shirt. An arc of electricity pulsated between them, making her achingly aware of his nearness. She couldn't help but notice how broad his shoulders were and how solid he seemed as the fluid movements of the dance brought them close enough for him to brush against her thighs, her stomach and her breasts.

Swaying to the music, they circled slowly, the tempo captivating her as she stared up into his perfectly sculptured face. Her breasts tightened as his inexorable hold drew her against the solidness of his body, his broad hands against her hips, cool through the thin silk of her dress.

"It's been entirely too long," he said quietly, his gaze holding hers as they moved together. A hint of longing flitted across his eyes before he shuttered them with a sweep of short black lashes. Her imagination. They'd only just met. Barely exchanged a handful of words, yet longing welled up inside her like a physical ache.

Yes, it had been too long since I've been with someone like this. She gave herself a mental shake. *I've never been with a man like this. Never. Not even close.*

Eva narrowed her eyes as if it would help her read his enigmatic thoughts. "I don't believe we've met before."

"It's been too long since you've danced like this." His words, the vibration of them, only intensified the ache.

He was right, of course. There'd been no reason to want to dance this closely to anyone for a very long time. Which was part of the reason she'd agreed to come tonight. She wanted to have fun, she just didn't want to fall for anyone like Kevin, who couldn't handle the truth.

She took as deep a breath as she could manage. *Relax, Eva. Just go with the moment.* She found herself so wholly hypnotized by his manner, his very maleness, that for a moment the sounds and crowds of the club seemed to vanish into a white swirling mist, leaving the two of them floating alone with the music. His golden gaze locked on her, and a shimmer of recognition hit her hard, making her chest ache with longing.

The cool stroke of his hand up her back brought a tumble of memories of their naked bodies entwined on a wide, sheet-rumpled bed. Of a sunlit hill under a cloudless blue sky, where the stroke of his hand and the scent of the long grasses danced at the edge of her memories. She could almost feel the brush of his mouth against her breast as a boat rocked them to sleep, their bodies slick with sweat—

Stop! My God. She didn't even know his last name. Her imagination was filling in a picture of two lovers that had never been.

But...

Some time, *somewhere* in the back corner of her memories, he was there. She couldn't place where she'd known him or how they'd crossed paths, perhaps as little as passing each other in the hall at the firm, or standing across from each other at the gas pump, but she had met him before. How she could fail to remember this stunning man eluded her.

But it didn't matter, any of it. They were dancing, and the feel of his hand, strong and firm at the base of her spine, their hips rocking against each other as her arms wound around his neck, somehow melted all Eva's self-control. She wished she could climb inside his tailored jacket, slip beneath the crisp white surface of his shirt to feel the heat of his bare skin against hers.

She'd spread her hands along what had to be a magnificent chest, letting her fingers roam and tease the ridges of his stomach and then curve around the swell of his biceps and muscular shoulders.

His fingers gently traced the curve of her cheek, beneath the shell of her ear and then trailed down her neck. "I wish I could hold you like this forever." The whisper of his breath just beneath her ear sent delicious shivers from her nape down to the apex of her thighs. Outside, the clock in the square began to chime ten.

And then reality returned, all of it at once: the noise and gyrating bodies on the dance floor, the beat of the music as the song changed to a hip-grinding rhythm, and the strobe of the lights flashing above the dance floor. As if they had never really been alone at all.

Raphael pulled her from the dance floor, still holding gently, but firmly, to her hand. "I have to go to another party. But I'm not ready to leave you yet. Would you come with me? It's purely a social call I have to make. Then, perhaps, we could go out for a bite." His sexy smile could strip the chastity belt off a nun.

The timbre of his voice echoed faintly as a memory. *Je t'aime mon amour.* Candlelight, the smell of the Seine through the open casement window. How did she know it was the Seine? She'd never been to Paris.

Warning bells went off in her head. He set off so many sparks in her, it wouldn't surprise her if people thought the midnight fireworks had started early.

She shouldn't. Eva logically knew better than to leave with him. If she let go with him, and God knew she wanted to, it could do something a lot worse than tank her career. She didn't really know him. But even deeper, some part of her heart thudded, telling her the truth.

She knew this man. Knew him as well as she knew herself. Gut-deep she was positive she'd met him before, and recognized him now as someone different, someone special to her.

"Come with me, darling Eva."

It wasn't in her power to deny him.

Anything.

CHAPTER TWO

OUTSIDE the costume party, colorful chaos reigned the night. Beads flew, music poured out of nearly every open door, and people pushed in a moving, breathing tide in the streets.

But it meant nothing to Raphael. All that mattered was Eva. He kept hold of her hand, feeling each pulse beat beneath his fingers in a maddening tattoo, as he pulled her behind him through the revelers.

The door to a black stretch limo opened and he helped her inside, choosing purposely to sit across from her.

He had to.

She was simply too much temptation for him to take the risk of sitting too close. As it was, he had to pull his gaze away from the rapid pulse at the base of her pale, slender throat. The mouthwatering sight echoed a deep bass, thumping through his chest, as if he were standing next to a large speaker at a concert. The moment the door shut, the frantic noise outside lessened. He watched Eva's pulse slow.

"Crazy crowd." He smiled at her, hoping to ease the confusion and uncertainty he sensed in her.

"What else can you expect? It's Mardi Gras."

"Well, the party we're going to is a bit more sedate."

"Family crowd?"

"Yes, but not small, by any means. All my extended family comes in from all over the world for the event."

She reached for the door handle. As if he'd allow her to leap out of the slowly moving vehicle. "Oh," she breathed, sounding almost relieved that she had an excuse to leave him. "A family reunion? I probably shouldn't go then."

He smiled. He'd never let her go. Not again. "They'll welcome you with open arms." Especially since she was the sacrifice that would save them all. But he didn't need to reveal that to her; he only needed to get her back to the estate for the midnight ceremony.

Eva might be confused on how she knew him, but Raphael knew only too well. While the scent of her blood had driven him across the globe to find her this night, the connection he'd recognized the moment he'd stared into those beautiful blue eyes had razored him to the core. More immortal than time, Eva—the soul that was Eva in this life—was none other than his beloved Isabeau come back to him.

The realization had been both divine elation and ultimate torture. She was so close; he wanted to crush her to him. But in her fragile human form, she'd die, again. How could the universe be so cruel as to ask him to sacrifice the one soul with whom he shared a bond for the survival of his kind—not once, but twice in his interminable existence?

How many millennia had he performed the steps of this dance to save his kind? And yet to save them all, he had sacrificed her before—and would again.

But the very human urge to kiss her, to hold her against him and feel the heat of her body, warred with his need for survival. He'd vowed when he lost Isabeau he'd never allow himself to be seduced by the sacrifice again. He had ached for too many centuries and, even now, felt as if his stone-still heart had fractured and was beginning to crumble within his chest. Eva bit her lip; the rosy blush it caused made him ache and burn.

"Why do I feel like I know you?" Her gaze raked over him, and he felt the temperature kick up a notch as she blushed.

Raphael cleared his throat, trying to ease the discomfort and intense thirst and hunger she created in him. It was like offering up a prime rib to a starving man and asking him to ignore it. Had he not been on so important, so critical a mission, or damn it, had even a little more time, he would have given her the most incredible experience of her life, and drank enough to sample the elixir she so carelessly flaunted before him every time her skin became pink and flushed.

He pinned his gaze on her, willing her to believe him. "We've met before. You just don't remember me. But I could never forget you."

Eva leaned forward, her breath shallow, the shadowed valley between her breasts alive with her heat, her scent. Raphael gripped the edge of his seat so hard he punctured the leather with his fingertips.

"Why don't you come sit by me?" She rubbed her fingers across the surface of the seat by her, and the amplified rasping sound it made in his ultra-sensitive ears raked over him as though she brushed his skin.

Damn them for making me choose. Wait—a mirthless chuckle rose in his chest and was instantly crushed— they were already damned, all of them. He most of all. He was the hunter, the finder, the seeker. The one to bring in the sacrifice to the slaughter.

He shook the morose thought from his head. For just this moment, there could be just him and her. For whatever reason, the universe had returned Isabeau to him. He dared not question why.

Raphael waited until he had himself under control before he shifted seats in the moving vehicle. The lights of the city, the jostle and noise of the drunken masses outside become nothing more than streaks of color. The heat radiating from her was like sitting out in the blazing sun, warming him like nothing else had in six thousand years.

Looking into the pale blue of her eyes, he found his desire mirrored back to him. It wiped everything from his mind but her scent, her heat and the sparkling champagne-like essence that was uniquely Isabeau Montfort, now Evaline St. Croix.

How could he have not known until now that she had been reborn? Only her scent had called to him once they approached the time of transformation. Had he known it was her he hunted, he might have refused. Refused and let all his kind die. Not likely. In his place Janus would have hunted her down.

When he'd met Isabeau, she'd been a charming mortal plaything. At first their relationship had entertained him, but it quickly grew, consuming him as nothing had since his changing. All of it had come crashing down the night her scent began to change to that of the sacrifice. He'd known, just days before she died, that she was the one.

It had made every minute all the more precious to know how quickly he would lose her. He'd tried to give her a lifetime of bliss in that few days. And he'd paid dearly for the next thousand years, hating his endless life and nearly losing his sanity.

Next to him, Eva swallowed, and he watched the movement in her throat. Just. One. Taste. Need clawed, tore, leaving him to gather his shredded self-control together.

"I've never met anyone like you." The raw needy timbre of her voice echoed his own insatiable desire to have her.

He smiled with difficulty. "And you likely never will."

Her pupils dilated, becoming wider, darker, sucking him in. "Would you think less of me if I told you how much I want you to kiss me?"

Damn, it was a good thing he didn't need to breathe. He wouldn't have been able to. All the reserve inside him crumbled. Raphael stroked her face with the back of his fingers, exultant that for the moment, she was his and his alone.

"Eva, my darling, you are the one I've waited for."

She blushed prettily, but all it did was inflame him further, making the desire to have her as his own, without sacrificing her, akin to physical pain, leagues beyond his deepest thirst.

"How can you say that, when you don't even know me?"

"Because here—" he pointed to his chest, with its granite heart "—I know."

Her breathing changed, becoming fast little puffs, and her eyes half shuttered by the fringe of long dark lashes. He moved slowly, afraid to frighten her. Afraid to hurt her. Afraid he might give in to the need that sliced through him.

But the moment their lips touched, he was the one carved in two. The fire of her split through him, branding him with her essence.

Together they were ice and heat. No wonder there was steam. Her kiss became more insistent, demanding he open his mouth, the slick heat of her tongue pressing like a red-hot ember to his lips.

But he didn't dare.

The venom that had flooded his system the moment he'd sniffed her out was already pulsing, aching for freedom under his marble-like skin. Vampires might be immune to nearly everything, but need was not one of them.

And he needed her. Like the blood that sustained him, but more. The spark within her, the essence that was Isabeau, Eva, reached in like a blazing light in the darkness, making it easy to forget the monster he had been for too long.

Perhaps death with her was better than an eternity of damnation? Perhaps if he changed her, she would bring that light with her. But could she transform him?

Her long fingers threaded through his hair, fisting in the long strands, holding him there. He could not let the venom loose, but he could pleasure her all the same before she was no longer his.

The thought struck deeper and sharper than any stake. All he had with her was this moment. And then this fragile bit of light would be lost to him again, perhaps this time, for all eternity.

He carefully pulled her to him. His hand skimmed over the bare hot silk of her skin, following her spine. She shivered, and his heightened senses heard every tiny hair lift on her skin, felt the shift in the air as her body shuddered in his arms. The soft, wet lushness of her mouth pressed against his skin, firing him from the inside out.

"Why won't you kiss me?" Her whisper so alive with her heat, it formed a caress along his jaw and cheek, her hands branding his chest as they moved beneath his shirt.

He chuckled, driven to focus on her, her pleasure, while he restrained the bloodlust beating inside him from harming her. "I *am* kissing you." He caressed her shoulder and her head fell back, exposing the throbbing creamy pink skin of her neck, each pulse an invitation to indulge himself. He inhaled, immersing himself in her scent as he trailed kisses from the tip of her chin down to the pulse that screamed at him for release.

Every hard fiber of his being fought for control. Alive and ultimately aware for the first time in eons.

Eva moved closer, pressing herself still closer against the solidness of his chest and arms. His magical fingers released the zipper and miniscule hooks that fastened her gown and strapless black bra, slipping in between her and the fabric to caress her sides and trace the curve of her breasts.

His cool touch, so smooth it felt like someone sliding cold satin over her bare skin, a direct contradiction to the liquid heat filling her, made Eva gasp, made her pulse and ache to feel his touch.

"I need…" But he was already there, the pad of his thumb brushing against her tightened peaks before she had said the words. As if he had read her thoughts.

Which made Eva's imagination take flight, as he caressed and kneaded her buttocks with strong, sure hands, bringing her across him to straddle his lap. The heat of his tongue, warmer than his touch, swirling over her breast drew points of light shimmering from all parts of her to focus on the sensation. She growled, deep and low in her throat, unable to stop the intense pleasure he released in her.

She rocked her hips back against him, aware of the hard ridge pressed intimately against her wet heat, then bent and bit at the skin of his neck.

He bucked beneath her, blowing out a harsh, rattled sound. The sound of a man fighting for ultimate control.

"Careful, Eva. Otherwise you may end up not having a dress when we get to the party."

She wriggled over the ridge, pressing down on it to sooth the pulsing need. "And why would that be?"

He locked his gaze with hers, his eyes hot molten gold. "I want to tear it off of you with my teeth. But I think I'd better not."

She licked her lips, smoothing the taste of him with her tongue. "Afraid I might bite you back?"

He tensed beneath her. He'd nearly grazed her delicate skin with his venomous teeth when he'd laved her. So close to taking his fix from her rich offering, coursing in the little blue lines beneath her pale skin. He looked her in the eye, carefully pulling her dress back around her to cover the temptation. He forced himself to focus on his duty to bring her back as a mortal. "Have you not guessed what I am?"

She seemed a bit put out that he'd pulled away from her. "You're dressed like a vampire."

He paused, then did something he never intended to do. He let the venom flow, ache and fill his mouth with its almond-like flavor, then pulled back his lips in a slow smile that revealed his elongated fangs. "I've no need to wear a costume."

He expected her to scream, to possibly draw back. She gasped, but her eyes glittered, not with fear but with excitement.

"I've always wondered if it were possible." She reached forward, her fingers outstretched to stroke one of his teeth. He grasped her hand, holding her back.

"It's not the teeth that harm, it's the venom. Best for you not to touch unless you are ready to exchange the life you know for one you don't."

Eva tipped her chin upward, leveling her gaze at him. "How do you know I don't?"

How in the hell was he supposed to resist when she offered herself so prettily to him? Duty. But if he sacrificed her, she would be lost to him once more. There was no need to worry about damnation when he'd already experienced that hellish existence of living on without her.

"You don't know what it's like. Difficult to want something you know nothing about."

"Then tell me. When were you changed, how did it happen? What does it feel like? How do you survive? All of it. I want to know."

Raphael wished he had the time to indulge her. There were so many things he wanted to say, to do with her.

Janus's voice intruded. *Time is growing short. Where are you?*

Nearly at the gate.

"You don't really want a history lesson now."

Eva's eyes narrowed. Determined. "I want to know."

Raphael sighed. It was only natural that, as brave as she was, she should be so curious. He would stick with the most critical facts, the things he had to tell her to help her understand, and skim the rest.

"Vampires are a far older race than you imagine."

"Aren't you immortal? That's about as old as you can get."

He chuckled. "I suppose to you it might seem like it. But no, we're not. Ten thousand years ago, in the time when men knew their gods, a wise man named Siphidius so honored the gods that they offered him eternal life. He took the gift, not realizing the bull-god who offered it would make him in his image, demanding blood sacrifice. The horns of the bull you see in Mesopotamia, in Crete? They are no more than the fangs we have in a different form. He drank the elixir of everlasting life, which we now know is the venom of all vampires."

She twisted her hair about her fingers, and he stared at the dark silken curl, wishing he could bury himself in her. Only her insistent curiosity and his duty to the others held him in check.

"Then how can you not be immortal?"

He leaned back, trying to distance himself from her so he wouldn't be so affected by her mere presence—as if that could do him any good now that he'd tasted her skin and felt her flesh. "Like I said, we're not. All gods have a breaking point. Over the centuries Siphidius became too great a king, wanting to conquer the world and become a god himself. It pissed off the gods, naturally. One doesn't ever expect one's creation to become an upstart, even though it happens all the time. So they sent a plague to kill the vampires, and it did kill almost all of them, save Janus."

Without being aware of what she was doing, she'd leaned in closer to him, her eyes bright and eager, curiosity getting the better of her. He wanted to grab her, but he dared not touch her again. Next time, he'd have no control.

"And it's come back?"

"Every thousand years, it is the same. Without a remedy, we age our true years in forty-eight hours, turning many to nothing but bone dust—wiping out nearly the entire species, except for those few who remained latent carriers to all their spawn. Only a marginal number of us survive, but the disease still lingers."

"How awful!"

Her face crumpled and a twinge of anger pierced his heart. Despite all the years, living forever wasn't as blissful as it seemed to those who craved, yet feared it. Friends and loved ones died away and too soon, in mere decades, a newborn was left alone, with only others of his kind for companionship. Love with a mortal was out of the question, unless one didn't plan to eat and was willing to suffer the all-too-brief existence of the relationship.

But this was different. Far different. Eva, the soul of

his Isabeau reborn, would claim his heart no matter how many millennia separated them. He was destined to be alone, knowing he could never be with the one soul who clearly completed him. "A cost for living as long as we do."

"But what about sunshine and stakes? Doesn't that kill you?"

"And I suppose you believe all that nonsense about holy water, crosses and garlic too?"

Her eyes widened.

"I thought so. You must forget what you think you know. Forget the silly fictional accounts you've been spoon-fed. We are dangerous, Eva. Much more so than you can possibly imagine. As much as I want you, I—"

"You already have someone."

"No!"

Her head tipped to the side. "Then what's stopping you?"

"My family. I need— *They* need you."

The dark blue ring around her pupils grew wider, taking over the paler blue. "You make it sound like I have the power of life and death. I'm nothing special."

He placed a hand on her, willing her to understand. "Oh, but you are, in ways you can't even fathom. We've waited a thousand years for you, Eva."

The rosy color that he loved left, leaving her pale beneath her lightly bronzed skin. "But why?"

"You are the only one who can save us."

CHAPTER THREE

"ME?" Eva laughed, hoping the nervous, strained edge of her forced humor didn't betray her inner lack of confidence. What if this was what she was meant for? What if she were hoping it was so much, that she was fooling herself into believing anything he said? "I'm an *accountant*. I crunch numbers. I don't see myself in a crimson cape saving anybody one digit at a time."

The golden color of his eyes deepened, darkened as he scanned her features. "As much as I would like to simply tell you what you are—" he closed his eyes, took a deep breath and blew it out slowly "—I suppose the only way I can make you understand fully is to show you."

She didn't move, but Eva felt herself grow emotionally smaller in defense as tension curled and eddied invisible, but palpable, in the air between them.

She knew instinctively that whatever he was about to show her would change her life. And, as much as she craved a change, she also feared it. Although throwing this sexy-as-hell guy into the mix made it more like two parts craving and one part fear. Remembering the heat of his mouth, her breasts tightened and chafed under the fabric of her gown.

Maybe it was closer to three parts wanting to tear into his clothes and feel every inch of him, and one part anxiety.

The limo rolled to a stop at a driveway flanked by great columns of gray stone and a heavy, elaborately scrolled black wrought-iron gate. Through the tinted glass partition Eva saw the driver roll down his window, but couldn't make out what he said into the security speaker.

The massive gate opened silently on electric hinges, then the car moved smoothly up the driveway, shrouded from the moonlight by the arching branches of the towering live oaks overhead. The drive snaked in the slightly dappled darkness, past trees thick with hanging moss, and kudzu, which Eva knew overtook everything it could—nature reaching with tenacious fingers to reclaim her own.

She shivered and rubbed her bare arms. Kudzu was nothing like what was happening to her tonight. Raphael wasn't going to "claim" her. Not against her will anyway.

Had it not all seemed so surreal already, and Raphael such a distraction on every level, Eva would have felt more on edge.

As it was, she was still trying to take it all in, trying desperately to understand. But her mind felt fuzzy and her body tingled, as if she had a buzz even though she'd finished her only drink of the evening hours ago.

The dappled darkness gave way as the limo slid into the bright moonlight where an enormous white plantation-style home glowed in stark relief against the dark trees around it. Eva's breath stuck in her throat. She had only driven past the gates before, but never seen the house herself, only heard about it and the somewhat reclusive family that owned it.

It was beautiful. Far grander than anything she'd anticipated. She'd suspected Raphael came from wealth by the cut of his clothing and the expensive limo. But clothes and cars could be rented. Eva doubted that a house like this had been rented. Did this place really belong to him? It was clearly a well-loved house with its beautifully maintained gardens, evident even in the glistening light of the moon. This was a home. A home that looked as if it had been in the family for generations.

"Welcome to my home." Raphael's voice curled around her senses like smoke. Ignoring the shiver his heated look caused, she stared up at the house narrow-eyed. "If the party is at your home, why aren't you hosting?" What had he been doing at someone else's party when he had an event at his own house?

His mouth quirked up in a grin. "My family likes to pretend this is a surprise party, even though I always know when they are going to be here. So I indulge them." He held out his hand and Eva placed her fingers in his. His hand was cool. Hard. Safe.

Raphael opened his door and Eva slid across the seat.

The glide of his hand against her palm as he helped her out of the limo sent a shock up her arm, straight to her heart, making it thump harder in her chest.

Cool damp air brushed her bare skin, as hand-in-hand he led her up the shallow stone steps and across a covered porch. The front door was closed, but the sound of music and low laughter drifted outside on the crisp, bayou-scented night.

Heart pounding an uneven rhythm, Eva hesitated as Raphael opened the door. "Maybe another time…"

"Don't be afraid, sweetheart. These are just my family and friends. I promise, they'll all love you."

As much as I do hung in the air, unspoken. Ridiculous, Eva thought, as she reluctantly let him steer her inside. He hadn't said the words out loud, and she wasn't telepathic. Wishful thinking of course. And yet—

The longer she was with him, the stronger the pull. Like the tide rushing to shore, she was almost certain she knew this stranger as well as she knew herself. Impossible. Improbable. Crazy.

This attraction she felt for him went far beyond anything she would feel for a casually met stranger. It didn't make any sense. It was scary. It was, Eva thought as they crossed a vast entry hall, intriguing. Inside, the palatial home was even grander than on the outside. Crystal chandeliers and marble floors, silk-covered walls, antiques and priceless works of art were everywhere. Eva wondered for a moment if perhaps Raphael were part of some minor European royal family she'd never heard of.

The hum of a hundred or more voices talking in low conversation wafted into the hall, sending a skittering sensation running down her nape. There were lots of people here, but she'd yet to see a single soul.

"Would you like me to introduce you?"

As Eva looked around at her surroundings, she bit her lip and nodded, suddenly feeling too insignificant to summon a response. Raphael slid his hand along her arm, twining his fingers in hers, sending another spasm of heat shimmering through to her core.

She began to doubt herself and Raphael's stories about being a vampire, and all of the vampires being dependent on her for their cure to a plague. It seemed just too fantastical that she would matter that much to anyone, let alone an entire race. No matter how her heart back-flipped when he touched her, clearly there was more going on here than he'd told her.

Men, wealthy men like Raphael, didn't pick up nobody accountants and bring them home to meet the family. That only happened in fairy tales, and romantic movies. Eva gave herself a mental slap upside the head. Call it what it was. She met a handsome stranger who she was powerfully attracted to and could tell felt the same about her. She'd willingly allowed him to take her home with him. For sex. Wild, hot, fabulous sex. That was the sum total of his reason for bringing her here. Sex. Good old-fashioned lust. Not love. Never love. Love spelled disaster for Eva. At least that's what she'd been told by the palm reader. And with Kevin it had proven all too accurate.

Vampires indeed. He could have paid any cosmetic dentist to trick out his incisors like that for effect. How could she have been so blind? Likely, this was some silly party bet with his wealthy buddies, like college fraternities played on each other, seeing who could bring the most pathetic date. Maybe it was some twisted Mardi Gras family tradition.

But all her hesitations came too late. Raphael's hold on her hand was strong, and she seriously doubted she could pull away, even if she'd wanted to.

The moment they entered the room, the hum of voices in conversation hit an unnatural lull. The sea of faces swam before her. So many. All of them staring at her. But not like the best geek brought to the party. No, and this was somehow worse, they stared at her as if she was the most beautiful sight they had ever seen.

She'd never felt so much attention fixed on her in her life. Somehow, this must be what it felt like when those nightmares of showing up naked at work really came true.

Thousands of candles lit the room, their flickering light reflected in the mirrored walls of the ballroom, but when she glanced at her reflection, there was only her, alone, in the candlelit room, staring at the macabre centerpiece. Rising up in the center of the ballroom, on a golden dais, was a polished mahogany coffin draped with red velvet. Holy crap! What exactly was going on? She could still hear the faint rustle of their movements behind her, even though none of them reflected in the mirrors.

She couldn't seem to stop herself from moving in for a closer look. And this time, Raphael let her go. Her eyes adjusted to the flickering light of the candles as she crept forward to peek at what lay inside.

A human skeleton of ivory, almost glossy, bones, lay within, but that wasn't what made her heart stop, then pick up double time. It was the one difference she noticed, the thing that took her by surprise. Beneath the glimmer of candlelight on the polished bone, the skeleton's teeth were perfect, especially the elongated, pointed fangs.

"You are surprised." His voice came like a whisper against her skin. Eva pressed back against him, needing the solidness of him touching her, then she tilted her head up, looking into his golden eyes.

"I shouldn't be. You told me what you were. I just wasn't sure I believed it."

His eyes shifted from golden to dark amber. "I was honest about that, but there is something that is left unsaid between us." The glide of his tender touch against her shoulder made her shudder with need. "If you do this, Eva, there is no guarantee that I can control how the process will work with you."

She glanced back at the skeleton. "Who is, *was,* this?"

"Siphidius."

"The first vampire? The one you told me about?"

"Yes. And the first to die from the plague."

She turned her back on the skeleton, her fingers digging into Raphael's shirt, clinging to him like a lifeline in a sea of confusion and doubt. "How am I going to make any difference?"

He locked his gaze with hers. "There is a special cleansing ceremony that counteracts the virus."

"And somehow I'm the inoculation?"

How could he possibly tell her it was more like a sacrifice? "In a manner of speaking."

We must have her. Janus's voice pounded inside Raphael's head. He blocked it out, refusing to be distracted. "Darling Eva, time is running short. If you do not help us, we will all perish by this time two days from now."

Her pulsed pounded so thick and loud that it echoed in his head, and her eyes went wide, before she swallowed and blinked.

"What do you need me to do?"

He almost chuckled at the absurdity of it. His explanation would sound very simple, yet complicated his existence on every level. "You climb in the coffin once the ceremony starts and the Siphidius skeleton disappears. Then the transformation for all of us will begin. We re-emerge when we are healed and the skeleton reappears when the ceremony is complete."

"That's all? Then what's the big deal?"

Ah. Here came the part that sliced him to the core and ground the stony remains of his heart to dust.

"You die."

"I—*what?* You *mean* I become a vampire, right?"

It would be so much easier to let her believe that. He'd done so with Isabeau, watched her fragile human form disappear knowing full well he would never touch her, feel her, smell her scent, again. Yet this time was infinitely worse. Because he knew exactly how torturous every minute of every day would feel without her. He could let Eva go, but not without her consent. Not without her knowing.

"No mortal has ever become a vampire in this way. They have all simply...perished."

Her shoulders stiffened, and then she looked at him. "I thought you were going to turn me into one of you."

Raphael's chest hardened with pain that radiated outward from the region of his heart. "But that is a kind of death. You do not fear death?" Considering the lengths his kind had endured in order to achieve an escape from death, her reaction seemed alien to him.

"I don't fear the unknown. Honestly, I've been dead once already, and it wasn't that bad. It's not like I'm in a hurry to go back, but perhaps I'm meant to. All of you will die if I don't do this, right?"

"We will." He stared at her, the gold in his eyes dazzling. "How have you died before, Eva?"

Inside her heart swelled with gratitude because he accepted her statement so completely, unlike Kevin had. She glanced again at the bones, then held up her palm and gazed at it, tracing one of the fine lines that spidered across it. "For my twenty-first birthday, my friends took me out to a palm reader who told me that my life would change the world and love was destructive for me. We had a good laugh, went out for drinks, had a good time. On the way home, there was an accident. My friend

Kelly was driving and died. When I woke up in the hospital, they said I'd died on the table, then somehow come back." She closed her hand tightly and gazed at him. A flicker of fear clouded her clear blue eyes.

"That time I was gone, I went somewhere. I'm not sure where. It was all white and a voice told me it wasn't my time. They were sending me back because I had something important to do. My life was going to change the world. I've been waiting to find out how and why ever since. I guess now I know. I've known I was meant to do something more important, bigger with my life than being an accountant." She let out a rattling sigh. "Saving an entire race from extinction is certainly up there with big. Really big."

He could see her resolve encasing her like a cocoon and was awed by her strength and selflessness. She was the most amazing creature he'd ever met, and inside he was dying all over again at the thought of losing her. "Evaline St. Croix, you are a most unusual woman."

"There is one thing I'd like in return, though, before I do this, and it's not a last meal."

"Anything."

He could think of a thousand things he desired. A night by a roaring fire with her naked in his arms. An afternoon spent in the heated sand with the lulling roar of the ocean mixing with the soft moans and slick skin. An eternity to kiss her.

"What is it you desire?"

"You."

CHAPTER FOUR

RAPHAEL let out a long breath simply to steady his inner turmoil. A strong desire to rebel and steal her away from them rose up within him. But as much as he longed to keep her for himself, he, too, would die without her sacrifice.

"Before I am transformed, or die, or whatever is going to happen to me, I want to know what it's like to be with you."

Such a simple request. Something he'd willingly give under any other circumstance. But there was no time. Especially no time to do properly what she'd asked of him. That could take…lifetimes.

"All I can offer you is a shallow imitation of what could have been between us. It is hardly enough."

Eva wanted to laugh. He looked so solemn and serious. "I don't think you give yourself enough credit. It's what I want."

He nodded and held out his hand to her.

Eva took it eagerly, lacing her fingers with his and gazing up at his elegant profile. Her heartbeat picked up a faster rhythm, and for an instant, she caught the quick tilt of Raphael's head as though he'd heard the change.

They walked together hand-in-hand out of the ballroom, without anyone stopping them. She leaned into Raphael, suddenly feeling colder, as if she'd passed an open window. Glancing back over her shoulder, she stared at the others who disappeared from sight as they turned the corner and started up the grand staircase.

"They're all vampires too, aren't they?"

Raphael's golden gaze slid to meet hers, and his lips remained in a firm line. "Yes."

"And they've come for the same thing you have?"

"We are all connected, Eva. This time the virus has mutated, gaining more power. In the past, some of us have managed to survive it. Now…nothing is certain. All of us are seeking salvation from the plague."

"It could wipe you all out?"

He shrugged. "I doubt it would be any great loss to humanity."

Eva shook her head. "I'm not sure about that. There's balance in everything. Look what happens when a predator is taken out of any natural cycle—things get really bad for those that are left. I think the same might apply."

He slowed their steps, his mouth curving into a half smile as he reached up to stroke her cheek with the back of his hand. "Truly you are one of a kind."

Their footsteps barely made a sound on the thick carpet that ran down the hall, which was lined with gilt-framed portraits in stark relief against walls decorated in crimson silk. Eva glanced up to see a picture of a man in knee breeches, with a brocade vest and long-tailed jacket, and recognized him.

"That's you, isn't it?"

This time he grinned, exposing the sharp white point of his fangs. "Not my first portrait, but one of the more recent."

"Exactly how old are you, anyway?"

His eyes glittered. "Old enough to know exactly how to pleasure you, and young enough to find you absolutely intoxicating."

His head bend closer, his lips barely brushing the skin along her jaw, skimming a warm trail down her neck. "Ah, Eva. The things I would do to you had I the time."

They had reached the end of the hall and paused before a set of double doors. Raphael pushed them open and bowed slightly, gesturing that she should enter ahead of him.

A giant four-poster bed took up most of the room.

"Do you ever actually sleep in that thing? I mean it looks like there might be room for six, maybe eight."

"Let me show you precisely what I do here."

In the space between one breath and the next, Eva found that her long black gown had vanished with nothing more than the sensation of a gentle warm breeze brushing against her skin. Her breasts tightened instantly at the arc of electricity that raced between her and Raphael, even though he still stood nearly across the room.

She blinked, and he was right against her, lifting her against the cool hardness of him, as if she weighed no more than a feather pillow. Eva wanted to melt into him, but he placed her gently in the center of the very big bed and pulled back.

Instantly, the need to have him near her, touching her, grew overwhelming, as if their encounter in the limo had never stopped. The velvet of the coverlet was plush and warm against her skin, and the look on Raphael's face made her feel hot and tight all over.

"You are even more beautiful than I imagined."

She blushed, and his eyes flashed with primal hunger that was powerful, scary and exciting all at once. "You aren't planning to feed on me are you?"

He smiled, his fangs elongated, his body tense, the edge of his erection against his taunt abdomen plain for her to see. "Make no mistake, Eva. You make me hungry in a thousand different ways. But no, I will not drink tonight."

Her stomach contracted, and small shivers danced across her skin. She could smell his cologne as if he were on the bed with her instead of staring at her with those dark, intense eyes from several feet away. Eva suddenly had the sensation of his hands, cool and firm, cupping her breasts, his thumbs brushing against the sensitive curve. Her fingers itched to touch him, even though she could feel him.

"You know this works better if I can actually touch you," she said between short quick breaths.

He gave her a sly, knowing smile, and suddenly it felt as if he was kissing her, his lips warm and insistent on hers, the slick heat of his tongue running along the seam of her mouth. How in the hell did he do that?

"Close your eyes and relax," he said, the words stroking her skin like fingers.

She wanted to, but the tension inside was building, pulsing and driving her wild. *Relax.* The word echoed in her head. That was damn hard to do as her panties and bra disappeared into thin air as well, leaving her bare to the cool night and the sensations that were flooding over her.

How could he be touching her everywhere at once? That was definitely what it felt like. The warm wet heat of his soft mouth swirled over her nipples, making them ache. At the same time, the smooth glide of his hand skimmed down her spine and over her stomach, causing a riot of butterflies to erupt inside. Eva pressed her aching thighs together and sensed the firm grasp of his hand resting against her bare bottom, his fingers slipping against the damp cleft of her core, making her shudder with need.

Moist heat sheened her skin as Eva writhed on the velvet. She could swear she felt the slide of sweat-slicked skin against the length of her body, making her ache for release. She reached out, desperate to feel the solidness of him against her. She needed...

And like before, it was as though he understood before she even completed the thought.

Dammit to hell. Raphael couldn't resist her. As much as he'd tried to give her release without endangering her fragile mortal form, this was more torturous for them both, and he gave up resisting.

In an instant he was naked beside her, her heated skin an inferno that threatened to consume him.

She locked a hot silken leg over his buttocks, pressing him close to her wet pulsing heat, and he groaned in desperation. Her pulse ticked inside him like a time bomb, each rushing movement of her hot blood screaming at him, demanding he take his fill of her.

He clenched his jaw until he thought the bones might

crack, determined not to drink, determined not to harm her. She lifted her hips and her slick heat convulsed against him.

"Please. Raphael. Please—"

He growled, knowing his eyes had gone red, unable to control himself any longer, and sank slowly into her, letting the fire and flood of sensations—hers, and his—overtake him as he moved with her.

Nothing mattered now but the fire that licked and gnawed and roared between them. He felt her first climax rip through them both, shredding him into a thousand tiny bits then bringing them back together. And suddenly the world exploded into a thousand suns, and Eva was the center of it all.

CHAPTER FIVE

Eva was certain she had no bones left.

At least no mortal should be able to survive a bout of incredible sex like that. But somehow, she knew that there was more to what had happened to her and Raphael than utterly fantastic sex.

For the first time in her life she felt whole, as if she'd finally found the missing part of herself she'd somehow always known was gone.

Which made keeping her promise to Raphael to be part of this ceremony, whatever it was, even more difficult. As desperately as she wanted to cling to him, since the crash she'd believed that she had a destiny to fulfill. Her hand pulled into a ball, the lines forming deep creases within her fist. The line of her fate crossing and ending at the line of her heart. The palm reader had warned her never to fall in love. Perhaps this was why. She'd seen that one line ended where it connected with the other.

She could never have anticipated that falling in love would bring her to the brink of her destiny, but now that she knew, she could not turn away. Eva knew with a deep certainty she'd been born for this. The gods, the fates, whatever had been waiting for her in that white place on the other side, had confirmed it.

He still lay beside her, utterly still, his broad chest not moving beneath her cheek. His fingers grazed a lazy trail up and down her spine, causing delicious shivers across her body.

Eva savored the moment a few more seconds before she spoke softly, "We're out of time, aren't we?"

His fingers threaded through her hair with infinite tenderness, and he tucked her closer into his side with his other arm. "I'm not certain I'm able to let you go."

Eva sat up on her elbow, resting her chin in her hand, and she looked at his golden eyes. "Maybe you don't have to."

She felt the anguished sigh come from the very core of him. "If you do not, all my kind, including me, dies. If you do, you die. Somehow I fail to see how either choice is appealing, because I truly do not wish to live without you."

She lay back, curling tighter against him. "I wish there was some way."

His heart twisted. He pulled her close, wishing he were capable of tucking her fragile form inside of his immortal casing. "If there is a way, I'll find it."

You must bring her. The ceremony has begun. Dammit. Couldn't Janus stay out of his head, even now, in his last moment to be alone with her?

We'll be there shortly.

Come alone. We will send an escort for her.

Raphael's brow pinched together. Why did Janus need him alone?

"I've been told there is a maid coming to help you dress."

She looked up at him her eyes softening. "I'd prefer if you dressed me."

He smiled, but it hurt like hell. The last image he wanted of her in this form was of her naked beside him, not in some damn coffin, still as death after the others had leached the life energy from her to thwart the virus and sustain themselves. He brushed a kiss on her forehead. "As my lady wishes."

Rising from the bed, he conjured white undergarments and a white gown. God, it could have been a wedding gown, with long trailing sleeves and a fitted bodice. She slid from the sheets, her dark glossy hair delightfully rumpled. He'd remember that. And the texture of it between his fingers, as well as the jasmine and spice scent that cloaked her satin skin.

Raphael brushed light kisses up her legs as he slid the scrap of satin over her hips, cupping her bottom in his hands and pressing his cheek to her stomach. With infinite slowness, he pulled the silk stockings up her legs, brushing and caressing her smooth skin as he went. He held open the gown for her, and she stepped between the folds and into his arms.

Raphael's gut contracted. Need and sadness ripped him to the core. He showered kisses down her bare shoulders as he fastened the little hooks up her back. She looked like a damned fairy princess, and he was the monster that would take her to her demise.

Anger, hate, at himself, his kind, boiled up within Raphael. How could he do this? God. How could he not? "You are, as ever, the most beautiful woman I have ever seen," he whispered achingly against the shell of her ear.

Even though the memory of ever having a heart was gone, tonight he felt the phantom recollection in the tight ache in his chest. Phantom or not, the searing ache of loss squeezed at his chest and made his teeth clench with the pain.

Duty or love?

One he wanted; the other was the grim path he was forced to take.

He'd damn them all, if they weren't damned already.

Eva turned and cupped her warm hand to his cheek, making his heart-of-stone fracture. "I've never wanted to be with someone the way I want to be with you. I think I love you." She paused, a determined looking blazing in her eyes. "No, I know I love you. I'm not sure how or why, but you're already part of me."

It took everything within him to keep standing. He grasped her hand, took it in his own and brought their joined fingers to his mouth, and gently kissed it. "You can never imagine how much you mean to me, how long I've waited for you. And I will wait for you Eva, no matter how long. I am yours, forever."

The door to their chamber snicked open, and they both started. A woman with long dark hair entered, nodding to Raphael.

He caught Eva's gaze and saw the fear creeping in. "Marie will bring you down to the ceremony, *cherie*. Never forget that I am yours."

Each step down the broad staircase felt like another step closer to the guillotine. When he reached the ballroom, the silent crowd was assembled, waiting.

Raphael stared at the coffin as the gong sounded and Janus appeared, his skin almost alabaster beneath the trailing black cloak and the shock of white hair worn long down his back. Raphael locked gazes with the elder vampire, whose eyes glowed red.

Janus's lips did not move, but the words were uttered all the same in Raphael's mind. *It is better to have loved and lost—*

Raphael didn't bother to hide his irritation and shot back his reply, glaring at Janus. *Spare me that twaddle. The damn fool idiot who coined that saying didn't have a clue what true love was. If he had, he never would have said that. The only true beauty in this world is love— without it, everything else is meaningless.*

The red glow softened slightly, but Janus's face stayed inscrutable. But this time he spoke. "Are you certain she is the one?"

Raphael leveled his gaze on Janus's impossibly smooth face. "If I could have brought you any other, I would have."

"Then you truly love her." It was not a question, but a statement, one that struck Raphael to the core. Even in his half-alive state, an aberration of nature, he was still capable of love. And if he were capable of that, could he save Eva?

"I have loved her for a thousand years. I doubt a thousand more would change that."

"You have sacrificed much for us, brother."

Raphael turned away, his gaze locked on the glossy bones in the coffin before him.

"The council has agreed that we will give you time to be alone with her on the other side. When the bones disappear, you will enter the coffin first. We will give you a moment when you can meld your soul with hers and take your sustenance without intrusion from the others. It is the best we can offer you in return for your loss."

Raphael clenched his jaw, his teeth grinding together. Certainly their offer was better than nothing, but it was hardly what he truly wanted. What he wanted was to die, too. The thought of once again living without her for another thousand years, possibly forever, was more than he could bear.

He stepped up on the dais, moving toward the coffin. The bones of Siphidius disappeared the instant he touched their smooth ivory surface, as if they had been made of nothing but mist. He climbed in; placing his body in the indentations the bones had leveled upon the crimson velvet.

An intense pull centered on his naval, as if he were being sucked inside out, his stone-like flesh bursting apart into atoms of dust as he disappeared from the coffin in the grand ballroom. Surrounded by the rest of his kind, Raphael had never felt more alone. And then, there was nothing but the white mist that enveloped him.

CHAPTER SIX

WHEN EVA entered the vast ballroom, the first thing she did was search for Raphael's face. But despite the hundreds of faces she saw, he wasn't there.

Somehow that hurt even deeper than she'd thought possible. Had what they'd shared meant so little to him? The stiff brocade of her over gown felt suddenly too heavy and the room too cold.

The sea of faces crowded in, making her heartbeat stutter. They all seemed to press closer and Eva was afraid she might faint.

A firm hand grasped her arm, supportive, but hardly kind. She glanced at the red-eyed man with long white hair whose pale face was placid, almost devoid of emotion.

"I am Janus, the elder of those gathered here. This

way, my lady." He led her up the steps of the golden dais, ever closer to the mahogany casket with the strange skeleton. But when she was close enough to see inside, she noticed that the skeleton was gone.

She turned to the man. "Where is Raphael?"

"He is waiting for you on the other side, my lady." He nodded toward the coffin.

Eva clasped her hands together tightly.

"It won't hurt. I give you my word," Janus encouraged.

Using the small step stool beside the coffin, she climbed inside, her heart frantic in her chest.

"God. This better work," she muttered, and closed her eyes.

True to his word, nothing hurt. Almost like having a heavy quilt tossed over her, everything suddenly felt heavier and heavier and Eva grew warmer and warmer.

Instead of being dark, the light outside her eyelids intensified just like before until Eva was forced to open them. The room was white, if it was a room. She really couldn't see any walls, or a ceiling. Just light, everywhere. And Raphael, standing there, waiting for her.

She rushed at him, flinging herself into his arms.

"You came," he whispered into her hair.

"You're here." Her voice broke with a sob.

"I have only a moment before the others arrive, and I must tell you something." He bent to one knee, and Eva found it all suddenly rather old-fashioned and pulled on his hands, but he would not be moved.

"I love you, Eva. I always have and I always shall. You are my life, my breath, my very being. Will you come back to me?"

"Come back? Aren't you staying here, with me?"

"I wish I could, but there is only a little time given to us on the other side of the veil separating life from death. You will meet each of my family in turn and they will ask the blessing of you, then they and I will return."

"Will I?"

He closed his eyes, and when he did look at her, the anguish etched into the planes of his face said it all. "I can only hope."

Then he kissed her fiercely, as if his entire being depended on it, and Eva held nothing back. But as she reached to lock her arms around him, he dissolved into nothingness.

Atom by atom, Raphael's body exploded outward, knitting together, taking shape. The snap of an electric-like charge skittered over his skin as the transformation was complete, and his eyelids felt heavy as he forced himself to open them. Reluctantly, Raphael sat up, pulling himself upright. He used what little will he had left to climb out of the coffin. He stumbled down the steps of the dais into the now-empty room and wept. All the others were already transporting to the other side and would reemerge shortly. It took only mere seconds for the transformation to occur, and yet it was that brush with death, that moment they touched life, that kept them all safe for a thousand more years. All but the sacrifice. If she did not return from the other side of the veil, she would be lost to him.

The ache inside him was nearly unbearable. He'd sacrificed everything, and gained nothing but millennia to agonize about losing her again and ponder his destructive fate. Perhaps he should leave them all, and venture out alone. The last time, he'd lived in seclusion for nearly four hundred years. That would not nearly be enough this time. He'd realized that his desperate need for Eva, for Isabeau, was love.

Raphael pulled himself together, sensing that the next vampire was going to reappear. He leaned against the wall and watched as one by one they quickly rose from the coffin, their bodies reborn. Safe from the ravages of the plague, they filled the room, but there was utter silence. All eyes looked to the empty coffin, waiting for the sacred bones to emerge to complete the transformation ceremony.

Raphael stood next to the casket, waiting. In the precise place where he had lain, the bones of Siphidius began to reemerge, seeming to appear first like a thick mist that grew more and more dense.

The skeleton was now complete. Behind Raphael the

gong sounded, ending the transformation ceremony that had been the salvation of his kind.

It was done.

Eva had not survived.

Why he had hoped this time, when it had not happened before, he wasn't sure. He just had harbored the one small sliver of hope in his being.

He moved to turn away, already shielding his mind from the others. Only the briefest flicker of movement caught his eye. It was as if a thousand invisible spiders spun their silk wrapping the bones of Siphidius in a white shroud that grew and filled out, quickly becoming flesh. Raphael gripped the edge of the coffin, silently willing that something different, something impossible had happened this time.

A murmur rippled through the vampires as they crowded up, jostling each other to get a better look. Janus pushed his way through the crowd and stepped up on the dais, standing across from Raphael on the other side of the coffin.

Raphael caught his gaze. "What do you make of this?"

The elder vampire steepled his fingers, placing the tips to his mouth, then he shook his head. "It is nothing we have ever seen before. So there is no way to know what will happen. The virus has mutated, becoming more deadly. Perhaps the cure has changed, too, becoming stronger."

If she had returned from death once, could she do so again? Slowly, a female form began to appear, and Raphael felt his granite heart begin to beat again. There was no mistaking the lips, the smooth curve of her cheek or the long lashes that lay in dark crescents on her pale cheeks. Eva had returned.

He waited for her to gasp, to take in a breath and wake. But nothing happened. The buzz of voices grew louder, like an angry hive of bees, disturbed and unsure of what to do next.

Raphael's gaze flicked to Janus. "She's come back, why isn't she breathing, dammit?"

Janus's mouth didn't move as his red gaze bore into Raphael, but the words came through clearly. *Just because she has returned, does not mean she has survived the sacrifice.*

Raphael tore his gaze away from the elder vampire and let it linger instead on the sweet form of the woman lying before him. He gathered together his powers and focused. Between his fingertips a perfect red rose materialized.

He placed it gently between her smooth hands, and realized with dread that there was no pulse. He closed his eyes, willing his acute hearing to pick up any trace of a heartbeat, any stir of movement within her body, but all was silent.

A suffocating blackness crowded in, drowning out the

hushed conversations of the others around him. She was truly gone. Again.

He opened his eyes to gaze at her current form one last time. If he was lucky, extremely lucky, perhaps in a thousand years she might come back again in another form. But even as the invisible vise around his chest tightened further and his throat burned, he knew that the waiting would be hell.

The petals of the rose shivered slightly. Had it been the air currents in the room? Or was it something else? He stared, thankful that he didn't need to draw a breath so he could focus. The room faded around him, all his attention riveted on her slender white hands. He saw her finger move, the movement so subtle no one else would have noticed.

Raphael's knees gave way and he sank down beside the velvet edge of the coffin, his face near hers. The thin skin of her eyelids quivered. It was all the encouragement he needed. He bent down to her, stroking her cheek. "Eva, darling. It's time to wake. Don't be scared. Don't try to breathe. You don't need to. Just open your eyes for me."

Eva could hear the hot silk of his voice, could feel the heat radiating off him beside her, but she felt like she was bound in a block of cold wax, unable to move, unable to speak, and she realized with a growing panic, unable to breathe.

What was odder still was that even though she felt the heightened tension in every cell in her body, her heart wasn't beating faster.

In fact it wasn't beating at all.

Eva put every ounce of strength she had into opening her eyelids. They barely opened. But it was enough. She could see his face beside hers.

Then she felt the crush of his mouth on hers, far hotter than it had been before. But somehow the kiss was different, more intense, flowing through her, setting off sparks in every fiber of her being. The cold wax-like sensation that bound her began to melt, making movement possible.

Eva sat up slowly, and Raphael's strong arms wrapped around her. Her ears heard each audible gasp of the others in duplicate, once in the room, another time in her head, like some strange echo.

A strange sweet liquid that tasted vaguely like almonds swirled in her mouth.

Eva.

Raphael's voice echoed in her head.

Smile for me.

It was impossible that she could hear his thoughts, yet somehow she knew that's precisely what was happening.

She spread her lips into a smile, noticing the strange sensation of longer teeth pressing at the edges of her lips. His eyes widened, and she felt him shake beneath her hands. He crushed her to his warm, solid chest, and it felt like coming home.

"Darling Eva. You've done it. I don't know how, but you've done what no one else ever has. You've returned as one of us."

I'm a vampire?

He pulled back a fraction, his face radiant as he stroked her cheek with infinite tenderness. "Yes."

This time, she crushed herself to his chest, a fierce joy filling her. She was going to have forever with him. And somehow, in sacrificing it all, she'd been given everything she'd ever wanted.

She pulled back gazing in his eyes. "What about the plague? Are you safe?"

"You've broken it, my love. I don't know how, but you've done it."

Eva cocked her head to one side. "I think I finally understand."

"What happened?"

"They sent me back."

"Who?"

"The voices on the other side. They told me I still had something important to do and I couldn't stay. And this time they told me what it was."

He smiled, and it lit the entire room, making her feel more alive than she ever had before. "And what was it?"

"To love you forever."

* * * * *

THE SECRET
VAMPIRE SOCIETY

Lisa Childs

CHAPTER ONE

IT HAD been a hell of an eternity.

Especially the past week. As he walked its dark streets, Conner West breathed in the scents of the city: gasoline and oil wafted from the asphalt; wood smoke and the aroma of grilled meats from the weathered brick buildings. From the people he passed, he could smell flowery perfume, musk and the sweet, coppery odor of blood.

He could have flown to his destination. Literally. Or taken the underground passage. But night had fallen, without a trace of star or moon, so the darkness suited his mood. Suited him.

Maybe it was time to leave the city, move on like he had so many other times. But he had friends here in Zantrax, people who could commiserate with his situation. His pace quickened as he neared downtown. Maybe

Julian would be at Club Underground. No one understood guilt the way Julian did. And Julian would never leave Zantrax, not while the mortal for whom he felt such guilt and responsibility lived.

But as Conner had learned the hard way, mortals didn't live very long, especially when they got involved with vampires. That was why he'd walked away from *her* a couple of days ago. He stopped along the sidewalk, at the same point where he'd *rescued* her from a heel stuck in a sewer grate. She had rewarded his *heroism* with a kiss. He licked his lips, tasting her yet…the tangy sweetness that was somehow familiar. Not that all humans tasted the same. *Miranda* hadn't. And *she* was why he'd left the innocent mortal on the street.

So he wasn't in to sweet young things anymore. She'd have to play this differently then. She'd have to show him who she was now; who he had made her. Undead. And bitter as hell about it. So bitter that she needed to destroy the man who had destroyed the life she'd known.

Despite the crush of the crowd and the volume of the music and conversation, she knew the moment he stepped into Club Underground. Her skin tingled, and her nose twitched as she caught his scent. Her scent. Even now, all these years later, he still smelled like her, like the blood he'd stolen from her. The blood she wanted back.

She turned on her bar stool and scanned the club patrons in search of his face. The crowd parted for him. Women gazed at him in awe, men in envy. Damn the man. With his golden blond hair and piercing blue eyes he looked more angel than devil. But she knew the truth because he'd consigned her to Hell.

He stopped, before he neared her, and folded his long, lean body into a booth in a dark corner of the club. People, standing because there were no other places to sit, blocked her view of whomever he joined. But she didn't care who he was with now...because soon he would be with her.

"He's not worth it," a feminine voice advised.

Brandi, as she called herself now, glanced at the black-haired woman who sat next to her. "You know this personally?" she asked with a flash of emotion she refused to identify as jealousy. It was just irritation...that someone might derail the plan she'd spent years formulating.

The woman shook her head. "Not like that. I know better than to play with fire."

Brandi hadn't known that...until it was too late. "He's that hot?"

"He's that dangerous," the woman said, leaning closer as if she feared his overhearing them even though he was nearly across the room. "He's reckless and careless. Men like him put us all in danger."

Us...

She was one of them now, one of the Secret Vampire

Society—a secret they would kill to keep. She glanced around the club again. Not all the patrons were vampires or other creatures of the night. Some mortals frequented the club for thrills because they suspected the secret. But they didn't know for certain; they couldn't know and live.

Was that why he'd killed her, or had tried? Because he'd suspected she'd realized exactly what he was…

But she hadn't known until it was too late…until she had become what he was.

"A little danger can be exciting," she told the other woman as she slid from the stool, especially since he was the one in danger. Not her.

Long fingers closed around her arm. "Be careful."

She patted the other woman's hand. They weren't friends; Brandi hadn't been in Zantrax long enough to make friends. Not that she would have. She'd left her friends behind in her mortal life; they were probably all dead by now. Of natural causes. "I appreciate your concern…"

"But you're not going to listen."

She had waited too long while she'd spent years tracking him down at every underground club in the world, so that she could finally exact her revenge. "No."

The air in the crowded club vibrated with excitement. Conner felt the vibrations in his veins, pumping hot and fast with his blood. He couldn't remember the last time he'd had such a sensation—such a sense of anticipation. Something was going to happen tonight—something that would change everything.

"Are you all right?" Julian asked.

Conner glanced at the concern on his friend's face. "Fine…"

But he wasn't. He hadn't been fine in more years than he could remember, but he'd made certain to never reveal his unrest or his guilt. He could afford no hint of vulnerability, for vulnerability in this society was a sure sign of weakness. And the weak did not survive.

Conner turned back to the crowd and scanned faces in search of the source of the excitement that pulsed in the air like the bass of the music. And he found her. He'd noticed her the minute he'd stepped inside Club Underground, his gaze automatically drawn to the sheen of her glossy red hair. But then Julian had waved him over to the booth before he could approach her.

Now she approached him with a sexy, hip-rolling walk that had his body tensing with desire…and anticipation. Black satin, in the form of a strapless dress, clung to every full curve. His breath shuddered out.

Julian whistled. "Here comes trouble."

Conner grinned. "Hell, yeah…"

"You don't need any more trouble, my friend."

He needed to forget the trouble he'd already found. And making love with a woman like her would probably make him forget his own name let alone his old mistakes. Tonight, more than any other night, he needed to forget… even if he risked making another mistake.

"Is she…?"

"One of us?" Julian asked. "She was talking to Ingrid at the bar."

Ingrid never spoke to mortals. Hell, she wouldn't even speak to the vampires who'd fraternized with mortals.

"Conner," a throaty female voice murmured his name. She leaned over the table, displaying a tantalizing amount of cleavage as her full breasts tested the bodice of the black satin dress.

Regret flashed through him. If she was one of them, Ingrid would have told her who he was and what he'd done. So why had she walked over to him? He braced himself for a slap or worse…as she leaned closer.

Her breath warm against his throat, she murmured, "I want to…*dance*…with you."

His body hardened. Maybe he'd only imagined the suggestive emphasis she'd put on *dance*. But he did not imagine the attraction he felt for this beautiful woman. "What's your name?"

Her lips curved into a sexy smile of pure amusement. "Brandi."

"Brandi?" He waited but she offered no last name, not even when he lifted a brow in question. Instead she reached for him. Her long fingers, with sharp red nails, closed around his hand, and she tugged him to his feet.

"Be careful," Julian said, but Conner ignored his friend's warning and followed where she led him to a dark corner of the crowded dance floor.

A throaty chuckle, like the purr of a dangerous cat, spilled from her red, glistening lips, as she turned toward him and looped her arms around his shoulders. "You don't listen, either."

"Either? Ingrid warned you to stay away from me," he surmised.

She nodded and stepped closer, her breasts rubbing against his chest. "And when people tell me *not* to do something, it makes me want to do it that much more…."

A grin tugged at his mouth. "Somehow I don't think we're talking about dancing."

"Is that what we're doing?" she asked as she pressed her body against his.

He swallowed a groan, again not wanting to betray any vulnerability or weakness. Something about this woman, despite her brazenness, reached out to him, eliciting a depth of attraction and emotion he hadn't felt in decades. Half a century, to be exact.

"There's music," he pointed out, having to shout over the smoky bass and the husky voice of the singer.

"You don't do other things to music?" she asked with a sexily arched brow. Like her shiny hair, her eyes glinted in the flash of the strobe light. Green with flecks of gold or silver that glittered.

"You really don't listen," he mused, both relieved and intrigued. "I'm sure Ingrid told you all about me—about all the bad things I've done."

She smiled and chuckled again, her breasts jiggling against his chest. "I know the bad things you've done," she admitted. "You've been very naughty, Conner West. Maybe it's about time someone finally punished you."

The flesh at the base of Conner's neck tingled, and not just because her nails skimmed over his skin. Julian had been right to caution him about this woman; she was definitely trouble. But it had been half a century since he'd gotten into trouble he couldn't handle. A person was fortunate, or in his case unfortunate, to meet his match only once.

Worried that he already knew the answer, he asked, "And you're the one who will finally give me what I have coming to me?"

Hell, yeah...

"I'm the only one," Brandi promised him as she pressed closer...so not even a fraction of space separated her flesh from the taut hardness of his body. Her pulse quickened then raced with excitement...and attraction.

She'd worked too hard for this, waited too long to be distracted from her mission...even by him. Especially by him. Heat penetrated his tailored suit and shirt, and her skin warmed until she flushed. With desire?

She drew in a breath, bracing herself to resist him and his sexy-as-hell charms. His blue eyes twinkled with fascination and mischief, and his grin widened, creasing his cheeks with deep dimples. God, he was handsome—insanely, unfairly handsome.

He moved, sliding his thigh between her legs. Her skirt rode up, but she didn't care. She didn't care about anything but the pressure building inside her. She was close...too close to her goal, to vengeance...

She couldn't—she *shouldn't*—think about anything but that. But she could think only of him, of the impressive erection pressing against her abdomen, as his leg shifted again, sliding between her thighs...back and forth across the heat of her panties. Her feet left the floor, so that she had to hang on to him, her arms wrapped tight around his shoulders. Her nails tangled in the silky curls at his nape.

Desire coursed through her, and she gasped at the intensity of it. Her nipples pebbled, peaking against the satin. The silky fabric caressed the sensitive points, as she longed for him to caress them. To caress her...

Dipping his head close to hers, his mouth brushing her ear, he murmured, "You're so hot...."

"And here I was warned that you might burn me," she admitted.

That wicked grin of his flashed again, revealing just the faintest hint of fang, while those devastating blue eyes twinkled with a sensual threat. "So you're not afraid to play with fire?"

Her heart knocked against her ribs, beating hard and fast with fear. But she blithely lied, "I like to play—" she stretched up his body, so that her lips skimmed across his throat, her fangs just scraping his skin "—with fire…."

He shuddered, but his hands tightened on her waist and he pulled her away from him. Her legs trembled as her feet touched the floor again.

"We can't," he said, "not here…" He leaned closer, his mouth pressed to her ear, his breath warm against her skin. "If anyone sees us…"

A vampire who exposed her or his fangs in public risked revealing the secret and subsequent punishment for the revelation. That punishment was usually death. If she could entice him to bite her on the dance floor, she could end it here….

Quickly. Almost impersonally.

Panic pressed on her chest, stealing her breath. She hadn't waited fifty years for quick and impersonal. She wanted vengeance—messy and personal vengeance.

He slid his tongue across her earlobe and then whispered, "Come home with me…."

She shivered, remembering the last time he'd spoken

those words to her. And just like last time, she lifted her gaze to meet his, and nodded.

He dipped his head and brushed his mouth across hers, briefly. But then she slid her fingers back into his hair and tugged him down again. She deepened the kiss, pressing her lips tighter to the curve of his. The smile left his mouth and he increased the pressure and parted her lips for the invasion of his tongue. He swept it in and out of her mouth, stroking it over her bottom lip, over her tongue, over her fangs…

And she was the one who risked everything, who risked revealing a secret she'd never wanted to know. She'd only wanted him…almost as passionately as she wanted him now. The temptation to take what she wanted, to sink her fangs through his skin and drink from his stolen blood…

She closed her eyes, fighting the temptation—fighting the desire.

He dragged his mouth from hers and slid his lips across her cheek to her ear. His voice ragged with desire, he implored her, "Come home with me, Brandi…."

She blinked open her eyes and stared up into the blue depths of his hypnotic gaze. That was all he'd had to do last time—to look at her like that, like he wanted her more than anyone else ever had—and she was helpless to resist him. "Yes, I'll go home with you…."

But this time things would end differently between them. She would be the one who walked away; Conner West would be the one who died.

CHAPTER TWO

THEY banged through the door, locked in each other's arms, mouths hungrily mating. Consumed with desire, Conner nearly took her right there, where he'd pinned her against the open door of his apartment. But common sense, just barely, prevailed, and he dragged his keys from the lock and stepped back. Then he lifted her curvy body in his arms and kicked the door closed behind them.

Her chest rose and fell as she panted for breath, her nipples taut against the black satin. He couldn't wait to get his mouth on them—to taste her…everywhere.

But then a voice, not hers, drew him from the fog of desire. "America's sweetheart, movie star Miranda Hamilton, was only twenty-five when she disappeared."

Conner tensed and glanced around what he'd thought to be his empty apartment. "What the hell—"

"Your television," Brandi murmured as she arched in his arms and slid her lips along his jaw. "You left your television on."

No, he hadn't. He had damn near thrown the remote through the plasma screen when this documentary had begun earlier this evening because the documentary was about *her*. Even after he'd shut off the TV, he hadn't been able to escape his thoughts of her. But he couldn't blame those thoughts on the television program. If it hadn't aired, he still would have been thinking of Miranda Hamilton tonight…on the anniversary of her death. He had been crazy to think he could forget her…even with Brandi.

He uncurled his arms from around her, so that the sexy redhead slid down his body. But then he quickly moved away from her and walked around the apartment, with its high ceilings, hardwood floors and bricked-over windows. He had to find the remote as the built-in TV didn't have an external off switch.

He checked out the mahogany bookshelves framing the television, even glancing behind them where he thought he'd thrown the remote. Not even dust lay back there; he hadn't lived in this apartment long enough to accumulate dirt or dust. Just ghosts. But then it wouldn't matter where he lived; she would always haunt him. His hands shaking, he patted down the cushions of his black leather sofa.

"Fifty years later, her disappearance remains an un-solved mystery," the narrator continued. "We still wonder whatever happened to Miranda Hamilton."

"Isn't that wild," Brandi mused, "that no one ever found he"

"Wild," he repeated. He knew where she was. Dead. Because of him.

Brandi gestured at the television screen and the por-trait of the young starlet. Even though the picture was black and white, it was obvious Miranda Hamilton had had pale hair, bright eyes and haunting beauty. "She was really beautiful."

More beautiful than any other woman he'd ever met—until his dark-haired damsel in distress the night before and now the redheaded temptress who'd come home with him. Just as Miranda had come home with him fifty years ago...

"She would have had a hell of a career," Brandi con-tinued, "had she not...*disappeared*."

Finally he found the remote, on an end table next to a lamp. Had he left it there? He'd thought for certain that he'd thrown it across the room. Hand shaking, he lifted the remote and clicked off the television. If only he could shut off his thoughts as easily...

"What do you think happened to her?" Brandi asked, her gaze intent on his face.

He drew in a deep breath, fighting hard to keep all

emotion from his expression. He could not reveal weakness to anyone, but most especially not this woman, who had promised to *punish* him for all his past crimes.

"What do *you* think happened to her?" he asked, wondering if she knew what only a few people did. Ingrid couldn't have told her; she had no specifics about Miranda, only speculation on his other sexual escapades. Miranda hadn't been the first mortal with whom he'd made love, but she was the only one who'd died because of it.

Brandi lifted her bare shoulders in a slight, sexy shrug. "I would bet poor Miss Hamilton got involved with the wrong man—one who broke her heart."

"So you think she ran off somewhere?" God, he wished she had. If only she would have run away from him...

Brandi tilted her head and pursed those full red lips. "I don't know. Do you think she could still be alive?"

Biting his lip to hold in a groan of pain, Conner shook his head. He'd shut off the TV, but he could still see the young starlet...in his mind. With her blond hair and wide eyes, she'd been considered an ingénue, but even before he'd met her, just from watching her movies, Conner had noticed that glimmer of mischief in her eyes and her mysterious smile. Miranda Hamilton hadn't been the innocent the rest of her fans had believed her to be. But she hadn't been worldly enough to suspect what he was and the danger he'd posed.

"You think she's dead then?" Brandi asked, her husky voice lilting with salacious interest in the mystery…and something he was too consumed with his own emotions to identify. "Do you suppose the man, the one she fell for, could have killed her?"

She hadn't loved him; she'd hardly known him. And he'd been crazy to think he'd loved her, that he'd wanted to spend eternity with her. He had never loved before; he'd had no way of knowing if what he'd felt had been real or only infatuation. Like what he felt for the flirtatious and beautiful Brandi. He needed her, for more than a release of the desire she'd built inside him. He needed her for oblivion. "I don't want to talk about her."

Brandi damn well bet he didn't.

He tossed down the remote, not knowing that it wasn't the one that had turned on the television to the documentary she'd taped. That remote was in her purse. His jaw taut with purpose, he crossed the living room in smooth, long-legged strides—as if stalking her. "I don't want to talk at all."

She didn't want to talk, either—not when she didn't trust him to tell her the truth. She wanted only her revenge. Then he touched her, just sliding his fingertip along the slope of her shoulder, down her arm to her hand. Goose bumps rose along the path he'd traced on her sensitive skin. Her breath shuddered out in surprise and desire.

How could she be so weak as to let even his brief touch distract her? But no one had ever touched her as Conner West had. No one had ever made her feel what he had. She wanted to experience that feeling again—wanted him—once more. Just once more...

He closed his fingers around hers and tugged her forward. Before her body touched his, he stepped back and tugged on her hand again. Just as he'd followed her onto the dance floor, she followed where he led...across the living room and through an open door into a dark room.

He flipped a switch, but the faint glow from a crystal chandelier that hung from a high, coffered ceiling barely illuminated the bed beneath it. Even if the antique four-poster hadn't been the only piece of furniture in the room, it would have dominated the space. Her gaze clung to it...as she imagined the two of them in it, as she had imagined so many times in the past fifty years...

She remembered the pleasure...and the pain. But in her mind the pain became his. "I like your bed," she said, glancing over her shoulder to where he stood at the door, turning the lock. He lived alone. Who was he worried might interrupt them? Miranda? "Let me tie you to it...."

He chuckled. "I don't think so...."

"I haven't forgotten—" anything, she thought "—that you've been a very bad boy, Conner West. I need to punish you for all your…misdeeds." And she needed to remind herself that while he'd taken everything from her, he'd lost nothing. His sexual exploits, with mortals and immortals, were legendary, but there had never been any mention of what he'd done to her, any repercussions from his killing her.

"Misdeeds?" He chuckled again. "Tying me to the bed can't punish me for what I've done."

It was what she would do to him after she tied him up that would be the punishment. She'd take back the blood he'd stolen from her; she'd take his life in exchange for the one she'd lost.

"It sure would be fun trying, though," she urged him with a smile. She grasped her satin purse tightly in her hand; inside she'd stashed silk scarves…and a wooden stake along with the remote.

He moved up close behind her, and his lips brushed her bare shoulder as his fingers toyed with the hook at the top of her zipper. His voice raspy with desire, he asked, "You're not wearing anything under this, are you?"

"Under satin?" she scoffed. "It's too revealing…."

Instead of lowering the zipper, he turned her to face him. But rather than looking at her body, he stared into her eyes. "Your dress may be revealing, but your eyes are not, Ms.…?"

"Brandi," she said, "just Brandi."

His lips curved into a faint version of his wicked grin. "You're not *just* anything…."

Brandi's breath shuddered out of her lungs in a shaky sigh. He was looking at her exactly as he had looked at her fifty years ago…as if he really saw her. Millions of people had watched her on the silver screen, but no one had actually seen her…until he had. He'd looked deeper than her sophisticated outward appearance and he'd recognized the insecure foster child who'd been abandoned and lost.

She couldn't risk his seeing her now…and realizing who she really was. She had to distract him as he was distracting her. After tossing her purse next to the bed, she reached between them and touched the tab of his zipper…at his fly. Long, hard flesh strained against the material of his tailored suit pants. She unbuttoned his pants and tugged down the zipper.

He groaned, as his cock sprang free, tenting the silk boxers he wore beneath. His pants dropped, pooled around his ankles and revealed legs dusted with golden hair. He shrugged off his jacket and reached for the buttons of his shirt, dragging them open to the sculpted muscles of his chest. He pulled off the unbuttoned shirt as she pushed down his boxers. Her breath caught, with awe, as he stood before her gloriously, mouth-wateringly naked.

With his golden good looks and lean muscular body,

he could have been a movie star. He could have been anything but what he was....

But, at the moment, with heat building from her nipples to pool in her very core, she didn't care what he was—or even what she was. She only cared how he made her feel—that he made her feel more than anyone else ever had. And she needed to feel him.

She reached out, sliding her palms over his chest. His heart pounded hard beneath her touch. Legs trembling, she knelt before him, skimming her hands over his washboard abs and lean hips...silky smooth skin rippled over muscle. She wrapped her fingers around the length of his cock; it pulsed within her grasp.

And he groaned. "Brandi..."

She opened her mouth to tell him who she actually was as she needed him to say her real name. But before she could give in to the weak impulse, she closed her lips...around him. Her fangs scraped the smooth tip of his penis as she sucked him deep within her throat. With her tongue, she lapped at the beads of passion spilling out of him.

His fingers clenched in her hair, holding her against him as she made love to him with her mouth, sliding it up and down the length of him as she closed her hands around his tight butt.

"Brandi, no," he protested, his voice rough with passion. "I want you...." As he tried to pull back, she clutched him closer...with her lips and her hands, sinking her nails into the firm flesh of his buttocks. But he was stronger, and his hands grasped her arms and tugged her up. His cock pressed against her abdomen, hot and hard and damp from her mouth.

"Let me finish," she urged him, licking the taste of him from her lips, "punishing you...."

"You're not punishing me," he argued, his eyes hot with desire. "You're pleasuring me. And that's not going to happen until I pleasure you first." His mouth covered hers in a hungry kiss, his tongue sliding between her lips, thrusting in and out of her mouth.

Brandi's heart beat frantically as an unbearable pressure built inside her, tight and painful. She needed more than vengeance; she needed the pleasure he promised her. She moaned into his mouth.

And he pulled back again, teasing her with his kiss and then his touch as his fingers trailed down her throat, over the slope of her shoulders to the satin bodice of her dress.

Her breath caught as she waited for him to push the material aside. But instead, his fingers skimmed over it, stroking her nipples until they pressed against the flimsy fabric. Then he lowered his head and through the satin he suckled the sensitive points.

Her breath shuddered out in a sigh as the heat and dampness intensified between her legs. She pressed her thighs together as the ache consumed her. She could think of nothing but the release she craved even more than vengeance.

While his mouth teased her breasts, his hands skimmed over her body—down her arching back, over the curve of her hips and butt, down her thighs to the hem of her dress. He toyed with the material and her skin, sliding his fingertips along the backs of her thighs.

"Please…" she begged, trying to reach behind herself for the tab of the zipper. As she arched, her nipple sank deeper into his mouth. He gently bit the point, and a small orgasm rippled through her.

His fingers were there, pushing her thighs apart to trace the trickle of moisture down her leg. Then he pulled back and pulled his hand from beneath her dress. He lifted his wet finger to his lips and licked her passion from his skin.

"Sweet," he murmured, his eyes dark with desire as he studied her face. "I want more.…"

Metal rasped as he finally tugged down her zipper. The dress dropped, leaving her naked before him in nothing but her heels. Cool air rushed over her hot skin, but nothing would reduce the heat of her flesh until she found the release for which her body ached.

As she had done just moments before, he dropped to his knees in front of her. He lifted her left thigh, sliding it over his shoulder as his hands slid over her hips and up her torso. He cupped her breasts in his palms, his thumbs stroking over the sensitive points as his lips skimmed the damp skin of her inner thighs.

She clutched at his shoulders, so that her weak legs wouldn't fail her, causing her to fall.

His mouth moved, his tongue easing through her folds of sensitive skin—over the very center of her femininity. She jerked in reaction, pleasure radiating from that point throughout her body. His fingers closed around her nipples, tugging as he dipped his tongue inside her.

Her muscles tightened as the pressure built. She arched against his mouth as he thrust his tongue in and out. "Conner!" she screamed, as sensations blinded her to what he was. She could think only of what he was doing to her. The pressure spiraled, winding tighter and tighter inside her until she jerked with the shock of sudden release. An orgasm slammed through her, her body trembling. She tried to pull away from his mouth, but he held her tight against his lips as his tongue continued to thrust in and out of her wet core.

"No!" she screamed, fighting against the realization that only he could bring her this kind of pleasure. Only him…

He pulled back and stared up at her. "Do you want me to stop?"

"No!" She couldn't stop now…not when she knew there was more. So much more…

He lifted her onto the bed, satin sheets sliding beneath her back as his satiny skin pressed against her front when his body covered hers. Her leg still raised over his shoulder, he guided his pulsing cock into her. His length and girth stretched her, her inner muscles clutching at him as he thrust then pulled out. He pushed the glistening tip against the nub of her femininity, stroking the smooth skin of the end of his penis over her nub—again and again.

She writhed beneath him then reached for him, sliding her fingers over the wet length of his erection to urge him back inside her. She arched her hips, pulling him deep.

Conner leaned forward, taking her mouth with his… thrusting his tongue between her lips as his cock thrust inside her body. In and out. In and out. The pressure built again, her body aching with its painful intensity.

His mouth pulled from hers, his lips sliding down her throat. His fangs scraped across her skin. "I have to taste you—all of you," he warned her before he bit her.

She screamed, another orgasm coursing through her as he spilled her blood then lapped it up. She reared off the bed—not in pain but ecstasy. Pushing him onto his back on the mattress, she straddled him. He drove deep, deeper than she ever remembered being touched before. But then it had been fifty years – not since she'd made love. There'd been other men—men she couldn't remember. Men who'd meant nothing to her...as she'd searched for him.

Only he had ever reached her like this, pulling emotions and feelings from her she hadn't believed existed. Even hatred; she had never hated anyone with the intensity with which she hated him.

He pulled his mouth from her throat and arched his neck back as he thrust his hips up, burying himself deeper inside her. Blood trickled from the corner of his lips. She kissed him, tasting the sweetness of the sticky liquid. Her blood. She had to have his.

She slid her mouth along his jaw, to his throat. Curling back her lips to expose her fangs, she bit him with a passionate violence.

He groaned and thrust faster, pumping inside her as she drank his very essence. Reaching between them, he slid his thumb over her clit—back and forth—until her world shattered.

She sat up and lifted her knees, so that his cock sank even deeper inside her as she licked her fingers with the blood she'd taken from him. Then she stroked the tips, sticky with his blood, over her nipples. He reached up until his mouth closed around the sensitive points and lapped up the blood she'd spilled. She shuddered and screamed, convulsing with the longest, most intense orgasm she'd ever had.

He lifted her from his lap and turned her over—then

he guided his wet cock back inside her. His hands tight against her abdomen, he thrust inside again and again until he tensed. He bit her neck again as he came, spilling his seed inside her as he spilled her blood.

Conner stared down at the woman in his arms, her pale skin streaked with blood—his and hers. What the hell had he done? What had happened?

He jerked away from her. "I'm—I'm…"

"Speechless?" she asked, tilting her head over her shoulder to meet his gaze. Amusement twinkled in her green eyes like those glints of gold the light from the chandelier caught.

"Sorry," he admitted. "I didn't mean to…"

"Ravage me?"

Ravage? That was what he'd done to *her*. Fifty years ago. He had lost control, just as he'd lost it with Brandi. But Brandi was one of them, one of the secret society. Miranda Hamilton hadn't been.

"I—I…" He needed distance; he needed perspective because for a moment there, when they'd been making love, he had thought she was Miranda. Her body had felt the same, as tight and soft. And she'd tasted the same: sweet with vulnerability yet with a hint of tart mischief. But it wasn't possible that she was Miranda. He had made that impossible because of his recklessness. "I'll be right back…."

His hand shaking, he closed the bathroom door, shutting himself away. He should have done that tonight, should have locked himself inside the apartment so that he wouldn't do what he had done—use another woman to forget about the one he really wanted. The one he could never have again...

Blood oozed from the fang marks in his neck. He tracked the trails in the mirror above the vanity as he leaned over the sink and splashed cool water on his face. He wasn't the only one bleeding. He'd bit her, too...as he'd lost control of his senses and his sanity. The woman had pushed him beyond reason...just as Miranda had fifty years ago.

And just as he'd hurt the young starlet, he'd hurt Brandi, too. He reached for a cloth and ran cool water over it. After squeezing out the excess, he pulled open the door and stepped back into the bedroom.

Even though the chandelier glowed yet, more shadows seemed to fill the room, cast darkest over the bed. She'd pulled up the blankets, so that he couldn't see her until he walked up to her. But even then the satin sheets covered her body and her face. He clenched his fingers in the silky fabric and pulled back the covers.

Shock filled him, tensing his body and jarring his mind into numbness. He couldn't react. He couldn't move. He could only stare down at the pale, dead face of Miranda Hamilton. Blood covered her throat and smeared across her cheek, even trailing into her pale blond hair. Her eyes, also pale with that unusual amber color, stared back up at him.

But her eyes weren't dead—they were vibrantly alive and glowing with hatred and vengeance. Suddenly she sprang up from the mattress, a wooden stake clutched tight in her hands. She pressed the sharp point against his chest.

Over his heart...

CHAPTER THREE

MIRANDA'S hands trembled as she grasped the stake, her palms damp against the wood from an ash tree. She'd researched everything in preparation for this day…when she would finally exact her revenge. She'd planned for every contingency—most likely his fighting her.

But he didn't fight. He just stood—naked—before her and waited for her to sink the stake deep in his muscular chest, to pierce his heart. A laugh bubbled out of her throat with her sudden realization.

"I can't kill you," she admitted as she pulled away the stake and dropped it onto the bed.

His blue eyes glittered with awe, as he studied her face. "You're no killer…."

"No, that's not why," she insisted. "It's because you have no heart." She, of all people, should have known that.

"You're no killer," he repeated as if he hadn't heard her. He reached out, skimming his fingertips along her jaw then across her cheek. "And you're no corpse."

She'd done her best, with stage makeup, to make herself look like death. Over the past fifty years, she'd gotten adept at disguising herself. She raised her hands and tugged the pale blond wig from her head; it was the disguise, a prop, as it had been fifty years ago. Red was her natural color...along with the unusual amber hue of her eyes. The green had been contacts that had been too thin to completely hide the irises.

"I can't believe you're alive," he murmured as he continued to stroke her skin.

She shivered. "You thought you'd killed me."

"Yes," he admitted, as he released a ragged sigh.

She reached for the stake again, closing her fingers around the wood. He might not have a heart, but the stake would stop him long enough for her to escape this time. "Sorry to disappoint you."

"Disappoint?"

"You must be disappointed," she persisted, "that you failed."

"Failed?" His blond brows arched as his forehead furrowed with confusion. "Failed at what? I don't understand...."

"And I thought *I* was a good actor," she mused with another chuckle. She had been wrong about that, too, she'd realized when she'd watched her old movies. She hadn't experienced enough emotion, until after Conner had destroyed her career, to portray her characters with any accuracy or depth.

"You are a good actress," he assured her, "*Brandi*." Amused that he would continue trying to charm her, she smiled. "Now. It took me a while to learn, but you gave me plenty of motivation to get better."

He shook his head. "You were always a great actress. In fact you should have won an Oscar for that death scene fifty years ago."

"Scene?" she asked, repeating just one word of what he'd said—as he had with her.

"Obviously it was all an act—playing dead." He pushed a slightly shaking hand through his hair.

"Playing?" she repeated, her voice cracking with emotion. "You thought I was playing?"

"Yes," he said, gesturing at her. "You had to have been acting because you're very much alive."

"No thanks to you." She lifted the stake and pressed the point against his chest again. "You drank my blood and left me for dead."

He shook his head. "No…"

Miranda applied more pressure to the stake. "You *murdered* me."

"You're not dead," he said again. Relief filled Conner. He cupped her cheek in his palm, stroking his thumb over the delicate bone beneath the silky skin. "I can't believe I didn't recognize you."

But he'd spent the past fifty years seeing Miranda in every woman he saw. So, in an effort to maintain his sanity, he'd blinded himself to any resemblances. "It was you the other night, too," he realized, "the girl with her heel stuck in the sewer grate."

"Yes, but you didn't take *her* home," she pointed out as if she'd been disappointed. "You must have lost your appetite for sweet, innocent young things."

He laughed now. "You might have been young, Miranda Hamilton, but you were never innocent. Or sweet..." The only sweet thing about her had been her blood.

Her face flushed with color beneath the nearly opaque layer of what must have been stage makeup. Heedless of the stake pressing against his heart, he lifted the damp washcloth he held and wiped it across her face. After washing away the deathly pallor, he eased the cloth from her face down her throat and removed the blood. Only some of that was makeup; the rest oozed from the fang marks in her neck.

"I'm sorry," he said.

Her bright eyes hardened with anger and hatred. "For trying to kill me?"

"I didn't want to hurt you," he insisted, "then or now."

But he had. He dropped the washcloth onto the floor and lifted his fingertips to the wound on her throat.

She tensed and jerked away from his touch, and fear added to all those turbulent emotions in her unusually colored eyes. She'd made love with him, but she was afraid of him?

"You came here to kill me," he realized, his heart clenching—not with fear, but regret. "And you thought you could do it." That was why she hadn't been scared to make love with him; she'd had the stake for protection... and his murder.

"I *can* do it," she insisted. But the stake shook as her hands trembled.

Conner wrapped his hands around hers and pulled them back until her crude weapon dropped from her grasp. While the jagged wooden point had scraped his skin, it hadn't drawn blood.

"You're not a killer," he told her again. "And you have no reason to kill me."

Her chin jerked up and down in a vehement nod. "You know that I do. You tried to kill me. You thought you had."

"I did think you were dead," he admitted, his heart clenching with all that anguish and loss. "And I suffered guilt over your death for the past fifty years."

"You suffered?" Her voice cracked with outrage. "*You*

suffered? You stole my life from me. You stole my humanity and made me into...into a *monster*."

Hell, he had deserved the guilt and still did. He had done all those things to her but one. "I did not try to kill you."

"So biting me, stealing my blood—it was all an accident?" she asked, shaking her head in disbelief. Her red hair tumbled around her bare shoulders.

"No," he admitted with an unsteady sigh. "I lost control. I never wanted anyone the way I wanted you."

She snorted. "Lucky me..."

"I'm sorry." He couldn't apologize enough for what he'd done to her, for what he'd made her. "I shouldn't have...but I didn't want to lose you. I wanted us to be together—always. That was why I tried to turn you."

"I don't believe you," she said. "I don't believe anything you say." But yet her gaze held his, as if she searched his eyes for the truth.

"I don't blame you for not trusting me," he said. He barely trusted himself around her. Because even now, even knowing how much she hated him, how she wanted him dead, he could barely resist the urge to push her back onto the bed and bury himself inside her again. "I can't believe it's really you...."

She shook her head. "It's not. I'm not the same woman I once was...because of you."

He hadn't killed her, as he'd agonized over the past

fifty years, but he had taken her life from her. "I was selfish." So selfish. "But I thought I loved you. I thought I couldn't live without you."

She laughed, but the laughter resonated with bitterness not amusement. "Yet somehow you managed. I guess all your sexual conquests helped you forget all about me."

"I hoped they would," he confessed. "I tried…to forget about you. But you were always here." He pressed his fist against his heart, where she had pressed the stake moments ago. "You were always here."

She shook her head, the fear back in her eyes. Maybe she was afraid that he was telling the truth. "I should know better," she said, her voice thick with self-disgust. "I should know what a charmer you are."

"I'm telling you the truth," he insisted. "Since you can't believe what I say, maybe you'll believe what I do…." Kneeling on the mattress, he joined her on the bed.

She didn't cower away from him, but her body tensed and her eyes widened. "I know what you can do," she said. "I know that you're good at what you do."

"Is that why you made love with me?" he wondered, unable to stop a grin from lifting his lips. "Because I'm good?"

She shook her head. "You're bad."

"And you intended to punish me," he reminded her. With a wooden stake through the heart? The endangered organ slammed against his ribs, but with dread, not fear, again. She hated him so much…and she had every reason to hate him.

Could he make her love him? Could he make up for what he'd taken from her with what he could give her? His love…

He touched her, skimming his palms across her slender shoulders and down the length of her bare back. A shiver rippled through her, and her breath escaped in a gasp. He clenched her hips and pulled her forward, so that his cock pressed against her flat stomach. The hard length of it throbbed against her navel. He wanted to bury himself inside her, to forever join their bodies.

But he restrained his own desires to focus on hers. He lowered his head to brush his lips across first the bridge of her nose, then the curve of her cheek. Before he had the chance to kiss her lips, she moved…and her mouth pressed against his, a moan emanating from her throat.

He swallowed her moan, as he parted her lips and slid his tongue inside the moist sweetness of her mouth. She tasted of blood, his blood. And hers.

She pressed her hands against his chest, pushing him back even as her hips arched against his erection. Tearing her mouth from his, she cursed him, "Damn you. Damn you…"

Her nails nipped into his skin as she clutched his shoulders and pulled him against her again. A smile curved his lips at her urgency, her passion just as intense as his. Maybe she didn't hate him as much as she wanted to....

But would she ever be able to love him...after what he'd done to her, what he'd taken from her? Her lips touched his again, and he shut off his mind. He didn't want to think; he wanted only to feel and touch and taste...every inch of her. His chest tight against her breasts, he pressed her back until she lay on the bed. Her legs parted, her knees lifted, so that her thighs cradled his hips. She arched, rubbing her mound of reddish blond curls against his erection.

His body shaking with the urge to bury his cock inside her wet heat, he pulled back...and focused again on her. He concentrated on her silky skin, running his fingertips over every curve and dip of her exquisite figure. She murmured and shifted on the tangled sheets, arching against his caress. He kissed her again, drinking the sweetness of her mouth...sliding his tongue across hers.

She ran her nails down his back, pressing him against her...rubbing the nub of her desire up and down the length of his straining erection. But still he held back, even as his body shuddered with the need for release. Instead of sliding his cock inside her, he slid his fingers...stroking them in and out of her slick canal as his tongue stroked between her lips. He pressed his thumb against her clit, rubbing it gently as she squirmed and writhed beneath him. He pulled his mouth from hers, letting moans and whimpers spill from her lips as she struggled toward her own release. While he trailed his mouth down her throat, he resisted the urge to taste her again, to drink her essence.

He continued down her neck, over her collarbone and the slope of her breasts, leaving only kisses as he skimmed his mouth along her body. He stopped at the dark peach tips of her breasts, tugging a nipple between his lips. As his fang brushed the sensitive point, her body jerked then convulsed beneath him as an orgasm gripped her.

She cried out and clutched at his shoulders and back. But he slipped farther down her body and tasted the sweetness of her passion. He teased her with his tongue, stoking her desire again until hot juice spilled from her. Her hands tangled in his hair, pulling him back. "You—I need you," she admitted, her voice cracking with the admission. "I need you to fill me…."

Her desperate words threatened his control, but then he realized he was giving her what she wanted. Him. And he guided his cock into her slick heat. Her muscles gripped him as she arched, pulling him deeper inside her.

He groaned, his body shaking with the need to thrust wildly until he satisfied his own desperate need for release. But he slowed his rhythm—even as she dug her nails into his butt and urged him faster. He took his time, fighting for control, as he prolonged the orgasm that gripped her.

She cried out and sobbed, tears spilling from her closed eyes. He kissed away the salty moisture. Then he kissed her lips, swallowing those cries of release. He skimmed his palms down her body, closing his hands around her full breasts and stroking his thumbs across her nipples.

She arched and thrust her hips against him. Then she reached between them and stroked the base of his shaft.

A groan tore from his throat as his control snapped. He grabbed her hips in his hands, lifting her against him as he pounded his cock inside her. She came again and again, her muscles gripping him so tightly that he exploded inside her. He lifted her and turned , so that he collapsed onto his back but she was still joined to him, still part of him. Just as she had been these past fifty years even though he had believed her dead.

But she was alive. And he had the chance to tell her what he'd rued never sharing with her. "I love you."

His words struck her with all the force of a stake through her heart. "No," she said, denying his declaration and her own instinctive reaction to it, to reciprocate it. She could not love a man she'd spent the past fifty years hating. "No…"

Her hand on his chest, she pushed herself away from

him, breaking the hold of his arms around her. If only she could break the sexual hold he had on her...

As she moved, he hardened inside her, spiking her desire for him, making her want him all over again... no matter the mind-blowing pleasure he'd just given her. Selflessly...as if he really meant the words he spoke, the words that warmed his glittering blue eyes....

"No..."

"I love you," he insisted as he shifted beneath her, his cock hardening and moving inside her. "I loved you then, and I love you now."

She gasped...over the sensations rippling through her with orgasmic aftershocks. But she shook her head, unwilling to believe him. "You didn't even know me then..." They'd had only that one night together—that one endless night.

"I knew you," he claimed, as he closed his hands around her hips and shifted her against him, burying his cock deeper inside her. "I knew who you were before I ever met you. Lost. Scared. Alone. I wanted to be there for you. Forever."

She shook her head again even as she moved, arching to take him deeper inside her body—to the place only he could touch. "No. If I believe you, that you were only trying to turn me and not kill me—" as she'd been told "—then you cared only about yourself, about what you wanted. You wanted me to be available to you. Forever."

Just as she had made herself available to him now. She needed to pull away from him, to break the connection of their bodies before another connection formed—one between their hearts and souls. She couldn't accept what he claimed; she couldn't trust his love.

But even as she fought those emotions, passion burned inside her…and the ripples of pleasure intensified until she shuddered with another orgasm.

He groaned and tensed beneath her, thrusting deep—once, twice and then he came on the third thrust. The warmth of his release poured inside her, as the warmth of his gaze poured over her face, his eyes aglow with love.

She wanted to believe he cared about her, but she'd already been a fool once for this man. She pulled away from him, separating their bodies. "You don't love me," she insisted. "If you loved me, you would have let it be my decision. You would have given me the choice of spending eternity with you."

"I was selfish and stupid," he admitted with a shaky sigh. "But having believed that I lost you, that I killed you, changed me. I know that what I did was wrong—that I should have cared more about what you wanted than what I wanted. Can you ever forgive me?"

"No."

CHAPTER FOUR

No. The word impaled his heart more effectively than the stake ever would have. She shoved the stake back inside her purse. Then she stepped into her dress and yanked up the zipper.

"You can't leave," he told her.

"Are you going to try to stop me like you did last time?" she asked.

He shook his head. "No, but it'll be daybreak soon. You can't be out in the light."

"I know all the rules of this eternal life," she informed him, her voice sharp with bitterness. "I spent the past fifty years learning them the hard way."

"I'm sorry...." He couldn't say the words enough, but she refused to accept his apology. Or his love. But he couldn't blame her. If their roles had been reversed, he doubted he could have forgiven her, either. So he didn't try to stop her as she unlocked the door and left him.

He'd thought her gone forever once, and he'd been wrong. Somehow he doubted he'd get that lucky again. She wouldn't be back. But at least she was alive.

How was she alive? He left the bed, rumpled from their lovemaking, and pulled on some clothes. Then he rushed out of the basement apartment. She was gone already. The streets deserted. The night was too late for mortals, dawn too close for immortals.

With time slipping away from him, he vaulted into the sky—flying through what was left of the night. Moments later he reached his destination and descended the cement steps leading down to Club Underground. The door was unlocked, and he walked into the empty bar. He glanced toward the dance floor, where he'd held Miranda—Brandi—in his arms. But he didn't linger in the bar, passing through it to the hall that led to another unlocked door. The studded steel creaked on rusty hinges as he opened the door onto a room that was cold and dark and smelled of spilled blood and death.

A switch snapped and artificial light flickered then flooded the stark basement room. The doctor stood next to the metal table where he operated or dissected. "I've been expecting you," the gray-haired man admitted.

He wasn't mortal, not anymore, but he'd been old when he'd joined the secret society. Old and bitter.

"Why?" Conner asked. "Why tell me that she was dead?" He'd brought Miranda here, all those years ago, when she'd been unresponsive. She'd lost so much blood that he'd been afraid he'd killed instead of turned her. And this man had confirmed that fear.

The doctor sighed. "Because she needed to die. How in the hell had you believed you could have a happily ever after with *her*?"

Because for the first time in his infinite life, Conner West had fallen in love, and that heady rush of emotion had clouded his judgment and his common sense.

The doctor snorted his disgust. "She was a *movie* star. People would have questioned why she never aged. At least they would have fifty years ago. The secret society would have been discovered. *She* couldn't live forever."

"But she didn't die," Conner reminded the doctor, whose dark eyes burned with madness.

"I was going to kill her," Dr. Hoekstra insisted. "But she was so beautiful...and so frightened and confused."

Conner closed his eyes on a wave of regret, imagining how she must have felt when she'd regained consciousness to a new reality. To eternity. "Miranda..."

"I realized I could use her fear to persuade her to disappear. So I convinced her to hide," the doctor explained, "from you. I told her that you'd tried to kill her, that you wanted her dead."

And she had believed the crazy doctor because Conner

hadn't been there when she'd awakened. He'd left her lifeless body with the doctor, believing the physician when Dr. Hoekstra had pronounced her dead.

The man continued, "I told her she needed to hide or that you would find her and finish the job."

Conner laughed at the doctor's failure. "Instead of hiding from me, she spent fifty years tracking me down." For vengeance, not love, he reminded himself.

Dr. Hoekstra sighed in acceptance of his defeat. "I should have killed her when you brought her to me. I should have killed her then."

Conner shook his head. "No. Except for lying to her and me, you did the right thing. She was no threat to the secret society. She's one of us now." No matter how much she resented being a *monster*.

"After tonight, after the documentary that aired, there's renewed interest in her disappearance," Dr. Hoekstra pointed out. "People will start investigating what happened to her, and we can't risk them discovering the truth."

"We?"

"The society," the doctor said as he lifted a wooden stake from where he'd held it below the metal surgical table. "You need to kill her for real this time, West. Or I will."

"I'll take care of her."

Miranda shivered at the icy resolve in Conner's deep

voice as he calmly assured the doctor he would murder her. Tears stung her eyes, but she blinked them back, silently cursing herself for being so weak that she had nearly believed his claims. He wasn't sorry he'd taken her life; he didn't love her.

She'd wanted so badly to believe him. Hell, she'd just wanted *him* so badly. Her fingers trembling, she unclasped her purse and reached for her own wooden stake. They hadn't seen her yet, where she lurked in the shadows of the doctor's underground operating room. Like Conner, she'd wanted answers. Hell, she'd wanted proof that Conner had told her the truth—so that she could return to his bed, to his arms…

She'd been such a fool. She barely held in a gasp as he reached for the stake in the doctor's outstretched hand. He might not have meant to kill her last time, but she had no doubts about his intentions this time.

Until he spoke again, telling the doctor, "I'll take care of her. I won't let you anywhere near her."

"Her very existence threatens the safety of the entire society," the doctor insisted. "She has to die."

Conner shook his head. "You're not going to hurt her. You'll have to kill me first."

"You would have been killed," the doctor said, "had I told anyone what you'd done, how you'd risked revealing our secret by trying to turn her."

"I didn't just try," Conner reminded the other man, "I succeeded."

She heard the surprise in his voice, and the relief. He really had suffered with guilt over what he'd thought he'd done to her. She hadn't had to punish him; she suspected he'd spent the past fifty years punishing himself.

"But turning her puts us all at risk," the doctor repeated. "The rest of the society will agree with me. She needs to die."

Conner shook his head. "No. They'll realize that she's lived as one of us for the past fifty years with no one suspecting who she is. They'll know she's no threat."

The threat was the doctor, whose hand held tight to the stake Conner tried taking from him. Miranda gasped aloud as the two men began to grapple over the weapon. Distracted, Conner turned toward her, and the doctor gained the upper hand. The stake pressed against Conner's chest, right above his heart.

Then a guttural growl emanated from his throat, and he fought back. But she suspected he wasn't fighting for his own life but for hers, knowing that if he didn't prevail that the doctor would kill her next.

"Get out of here!" he shouted at her, confirming her suspicion.

"No," she said, "I'm not leaving you." She rushed from the shadows, her weapon clutched tight in her hands. But before she could help, the metal table crashed over and the two men fell to the floor, locked in combat.

Another cry rang out in the room, this one of excruciating pain. Then silence fell, broken only by her agitated breaths. "Conner!"

For fifty years she had wanted him dead, but now she begged for him to live as she knelt near the tangled bodies. The doctor shifted, rising from the floor. And she tightened her grasp on the stake, ready to defend herself. But the doctor rolled over, as Conner pushed off his body. Blood spurted around the stake buried deep in Dr. Hoekstra's chest.

Conner stared at the other man, his blue eyes wide with horror. "I—I killed him...."

How had she ever considered him a murderer? Would he ever forgive her for doubting him?

He had become what she had thought he was—a killer. Although, hours ago, the society had exonerated him of any wrongdoing in the doctor's death, he knew better than to hope she would. And so he packed his belongings to leave Zantrax and her. Forever.

"Where are you going?" a husky female voice asked.

Startled, Conner whirled around to the door where she stood, her amber gaze on him. "Miranda..."

"Or Brandi," she said as she crossed the room to him. "I've spent more years living as her than Miranda."

He opened his mouth to apologize again, but she pressed her fingers across his lips.

"I see it in your eyes," she said. "You don't have to keep saying it." She stroked her fingertips over the stubble along his jaw. "You don't have to keep feeling it."

He shook his head. "That's not possible. I took everything away from you. Your career, your future…" And he would never forgive himself for acting so recklessly, so selfishly…

"My career?" She laughed. "I would have been forgotten long ago if not for my mysterious disappearance. I was a second-rate starlet. You made me a legend."

Confusion…and desire…filled Conner as she stepped closer, her body brushing up against his. She'd changed out of the black satin dress for a curve-hugging knit one in nearly the same red as her hair. "You were so mad at me," he reminded her, "mad enough to kill me. How can you forgive me?"

"I haven't," she said even as she arched her hips against him.

"Of course."

"And I won't…if you leave me," she said as she wrapped her hands around his nape and pulled his head down to hers. She kissed him hungrily, her lips pressing his apart so that her tongue slid into his mouth and tangled with his. Their fangs scraped, sparking his desire into smoldering passion.

He slid his hands down her back to her hips. He cupped her butt in his palms and lifted her as she tilted her pelvis, rubbing her hips and abdomen against his erection. A groan slipped from his lips, and his control snapped. He couldn't take it slow; he couldn't make love to her as thoroughly as he had before.

He needed her now.

Her hand pushed between their bodies, and she unsnapped and unzipped his jeans, freeing his cock. He lifted her dress and tugged aside her panties as she guided him inside her. She was wet and ready for him, her body moist and hot as her inner muscles gripped him.

Her nails dug into his shoulders. "Hard," she urged him as she wrapped her bare legs around his waist. She slid up and down.

Not bothering to knock the suitcase from the bed, he stayed on his feet, widening his stance to brace himself as he thrust inside her…as frantically as she rode him. Panting for breath, she pressed her mouth to his throat, nipping his skin with her fangs, but she didn't drink. Instead she invited him, "Bite me…."

He met her gaze, and seeing the acceptance and excitement in her eyes, he buried his face in her neck and sank his fangs into the silky skin of her throat. Her blood trickled over his tongue, sweet and sticky, like the passion that poured over his cock as she came.

All his muscles taut, he thrust again and again…and joined her in blissful oblivion. "Brandi!"

She smiled against his mouth as she kissed him. "I prefer Brandi," she admitted. "Not just the name but the life. I don't feel so lost anymore…."

In his arms, she felt just the opposite as that abandoned child who'd never known love. She felt as if she belonged…with him. To him.

"You didn't take away my future," she assured him. "You gave me one…with you."

His blue eyes bright with hope, he met her gaze. "Are you saying…"

"That I love you?" she asked then nodded as he smiled. "Yes, I love you. And I want to spend eternity with you."

His arms tightened around her, pressing her breasts against his chest, where his heart—the heart she'd doubted he had—beat hard and fast. "I love you," he vowed.

This time she believed him, not just because she trusted him now, but because she realized she was worthy of love. Her parents might have abandoned and forgotten about her. But in fifty years, he never had. Happiness filling her, her lips curved into a smile. "I know."

"I love you now, and I will love you forever," Conner promised.

She wrapped her arms around his shoulders, holding

him tight. "That's good because I spent so long looking for you I'm never going to let you go." She'd tracked him down for vengeance and had found love instead.

* * * * *

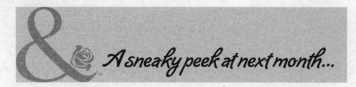

A sneaky peek at next month...

NOCTURNE™

BEYOND DARKNESS...BEYOND DESIRE

My wish list for next month's titles...

In stores from 17th February 2012:

❏ Claim the Night — Rachel Lee

❏ Wolf Whisperer — Karen Whiddon

In stores from 2nd March 2012:

❏ Embraced by Blood — Laurie London

Available at WHSmith, Tesco, Asda, Eason, Amazon and Apple

Just can't wait?

0212/89

Don't miss Pink Tuesday
One day. 10 hours. 10 deals.

PINK TUESDAY
IS COMING!

10 hours...10 unmissable deals!

This Valentine's Day we will be bringing
you fantastic offers across a range of
our titles—each hour, on the hour!

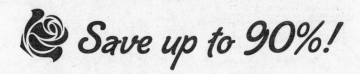

Pink Tuesday starts
9am Tuesday 14th February

The World of Mills & Boon®

There's a Mills & Boon® series that's perfect for you. We publish ten series and with new titles every month, you never have to wait long for your favourite to come along.

Blaze® Scorching hot, sexy reads

By Request Relive the romance with the best of the best

Cherish™ Romance to melt the heart every time

Desire™ Passionate and dramatic love stories

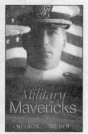